*Rachel
Thanks J.
Dearest friends, follow*

Sinz of
The Fatha

your dreams until the end of time and then some. Its better outside the lot!

Kirk Coleman *Kirk*

Milligan Books   California

Copyright © 2004 by Kirk Coleman
Lathrup Village, Michigan
All rights reserved
Printed and Bound in the United States of America

Published and Distributed by:
Milligan Books, Inc.

Cover Design by: Clint D. Johnson: CDJ Artistix

Formatting by:
Alpha Desktop Publishing

First Printing, January 2005
10 9 8 7 6 5 4 3 2 1

ISBN 0-9764690-0-6

Publisher's note:
This is a work of fiction. Names, characters, places and incidents either are product of the author's imagination or are used fictitiously, and any resemblance to actual persons, living or dead, events, or locales is entirely coincidental.

All rights reserved. No part of this book may be reproduced in whole or in part, in any form or by any means, electronic or mechanical, including photocopying, recording or by any information storage and retrieval system, without permission in writing from the author.

Milligan Books, Inc.
1425 W. Manchester Ave., Suite C
Los Angeles, California 90047
www.milliganbooks.com
(323) 750-3592

Dedication

This book is dedicated to the One, mighty and merciful, who gives light to saint and sinner alike. It is also dedicated to Ludeal Coleman, my mother and friend, a spiritual lighthouse of wisdom and vision and to DeMal and Dad—may you live forever in the pages of this book and in me. And to the dreamer ... oh beautiful dreamer!—builder of civilizations yet seen and composer of music yet heard. Dream on ....

About The Author

Kirk Coleman is a writer from Detroit, Michigan, who has studied, worked, lived, and loved on both sides of the Mason-Dixon Line. A graduate of Detroit's historic Cass Tech. H.S., he holds an English/Social Science degree with equal, combined credits from Morehouse (Baptist) and Marygrove (Catholic) colleges —64 each. Once selected over 150 other applicants for a nationwide job search for the <u>Atlanta Journal Constitution</u> newspaper, he attributes his selection to timing and humility. A modern-day Renaissance man, he has worked for years in corporate sales, marketing, and distribution, as well as 5 years in teaching with Ferndale schools while running two separate businesses. He is married and currently works for the State of Michigan.

Prologue

It just couldn't be over, I thought as my brother Jim and I bounded up the concrete stairs past two middle-aged white men in black suits propping up the door like sentry soldiers. The church, which stood forty yards off the road on a sloped hill, faded into a backdrop of pines and weeping willows. The somber atmosphere washed over me, alerting me something was amiss, but at first I couldn't pinpoint what was wrong.

From years of experience, I expected the loud singing, the drama, the histrionics of a black funeral, but to my surprise, sedate organ music wafted throughout the sanctuary. Although this seemed unusual, that wasn't what bothered me.

The church's architecture was simple and nonthreatening, unlike a massive cathedral or an urban church that must expand to keep up with its growing membership. A modest steeple towered above the simple wooden church, and although it appeared neat and well maintained, it would have benefited from a coat of fresh white paint, although I didn't notice it then.

Although traditional chrysanthemums were present, they were diluted by the smell of sweat, cologne, and all that comes when one hundred people are squeezed into a 25- by 40-foot area. Some people casually strolled in and out of the doorway, making no excuse for their actions, wiping their brows and fanning themselves. In the tradition of Southern hospitality, the open door seemed to welcome us warmly, but at the same time, its oak frame exuded a simplicity that seemed timeless.

I, again, took notice of the two white men standing at the door, trying to figure them out.

They must be funeral directors, I thought. Silently, I took this in and just assumed that the South had integrated. I recalled a time when white funeral homes would not bury blacks.

Abruptly, the solemn organ music in the background lanced at me, without celebration, almost as if it were silent. This was not what I expected.

Black funerals were generally part celebration, part going-home ceremony, and part pageantry of sorrow, but to see this one, you would not have known it. A picture of Jesus was over the back pew. Even though it was the centerpiece of the back wall, He (Jesus) appeared to look away, as if He was preoccupied with something other than what went on in the little church. He was undoubtedly white.

We nodded at the two white men as Jim and I trudged in. I could see the casket right in the middle where the long aisle ended in the simple, architecturally-challenged church. I could only hear the solemn organ music playing while I walked through what appeared to be a tunnel with a casket at its end. My senses accelerated. I could smell the heat and the mildew of the little wooden church that probably had not enjoyed such a large congregation for a while.

I saw the people, both black and white, and I didn't see them. I was on a mission. I just wanted to see the "dearly departed."

My eyes scanned the front of the church. The casket was still open! I heaved a deep sigh of relief. The mounted tension from this journey fell free like a suit of armor. Thank God for "C. P." time! This time it was in my favor.

Assuming Jim was walking behind me, I didn't even look around to see if Dad was there with any other members of our clan. I stared at *him* until I stood above *him*, keeping my eyes on *him* the whole time. The door to the past began to open. It was not that I had never seen this man before. This was my grandmother Jessie Small's brother. I had seen him at least twice in Minters, Alabama, or Detroit. There was a picture in the family photo album with him standing in front of the old log cabin house when he was about fifty years old.

William Small Jr., or "Uncle Willie," as my Dad called him, outlived his brother, Monroe, and my grandmother, Jessie. They all lived a long time, in their mid-eighties. My great-grandfather's other children from other mistresses were spread within a twenty-mile radius, but these three siblings had the same mother, Mattie Basket.

I carefully examined the man who lay there as if he were sleeping. Even in death, he looked good for a man of eighty. As I studied the large-framed man lying there, I could not help but think of my late brother,

DeMal. The hands were huge, graced by long fingers, which were possibly double-jointed at the thumbs, like DeMal's. The face was long, bony, and sculpted, like DeMal's face. The body, like DeMal's, was large and, judging from the length of the casket, probably once towered well over six feet tall. The hair, though sprinkled with gray, had been reddish-brown, like DeMal's. The likenesses were profound.

Willie Small, the deceased, his father, my great-grandfather, and DeMal, my late brother, were all somehow linked as one. I could see the transgression of my great-grandfather's genes in three generations, in three men.

Chapter 1

The cold rain washed upon the window in tiny pellets, beating away like a toy drummer on continuous rounds, washing away the salt and sentiment of a Detroit winter deep into the earth in preparation for spring. I turned over, adjusting my pillow and thoughts, choosing sleep over consciousness with all its benefits. For all I knew, it could have been snow this April morning, although I longed for warmer days ahead. In Detroit it was not good to rush the seasons. People in Michigan know that the seasons change in time, their own, sometimes overlapping the other with little announcement. Today I would sleep in until I was awakened. It seemed as if my energy came from the sun, which, today, was hidden deep behind the clouds. It was a perfect day to sleep and shut the world out. This is what I wanted to do, at least for a while. Then the phone rang interrupting it all.

Jim called me about 7:30 Friday morning on one of the coolest, rainiest days of early spring. One more ring and the machine would have picked up the call as I grabbed the telephone in the dark.

"Yeah-llo.

"Hey, Kirk, still want to go?" Jim's voice sounded terse and eager.

"Umm-ahh-wow, I don't know," I growled in my morning voice. "Who are you going with?" I tried to evade what I already knew was coming.

"I thought we were going to go," he said.

Ah, I knew it. I thought that since he didn't confirm with me the night before that the trip was off, that he could or should have given me more than a few hours notice to get ready—oh well! I couldn't let him drive that far on his own.

"If we go, I absolutely have to be back Sunday for a 9:00 Monday meeting, and I have training all week."

"Hey, I have to be in at six on Monday myself. Kirk, I slept on this, and I woke up and decided to go because after this, a door will be closed that will never be reopened, and we will probably never see most of these people again," he yawned.

Taken by the truth and sincerity of this statement, I consented. "What are you driving—the minivan?"

"No, the Acura—I don't want to put the miles on my lease," he said.

"What time are you coming, because I have a few loose ends to tighten up, including the bank. Why didn't you let me know last night?"

"I wasn't sure. I had to check ..."

"What time?"

"About ten."

"Nah, man. The bank doesn't open until ..."

"Okay. See you at 11:00," he said.

"Yeah. You got a CD player?"

"Nah."

"Alright ... later."

"At 11:00 now," he said before hanging up, although I knew he meant 12:00.

I hung up, turned over, and closed my eyes while contemplating the journey ahead. As the pellets of rain continued on the windowpane, I thought about the purpose of taking the trip in the first place and was saddened. I closed my eyes and said a horizontal prayer because it was easier at the time.

"This is for you, baby brother. I wish you peace and eternal rest. Wherever you are in this universe, I hope and pray that it is one hundred thousand times better than this place, and I know it is. I know it is—it must be. I hope you get to see and do things you only dreamed of in this life. Peace to you, baby brother." Wiping a tear on the pillow, I drifted back to sleep.

When I awakened at 9:00 a.m., I hit the ground running. With so little time to get ready, my thoughts were scattered. *Okay, a suit, tie, shirt, socks, and one outfit which I'll wear there and back. Underwear, toothbrush, deodorant—okay! Oops, hairbrush, oil—all set.*

We met at Mom's house, which will always be home to me. It was the central location of family activity, where we all had keys, clothes, and belongings—me more than anyone else. The 2000-square-foot red brick colonial that once housed a family of five was more space than she now needed or could maintain. It was my duty to see that Mom stayed there as long as she wished, without feeling the emptiness of a once fully occupied home. She packed both of us a little lunch of turkey sandwiches with lettuce and tomato and a snack cake.

Each sandwich, perfectly wrapped and almost identical in portion, looked like it had rolled off one of Detroit's assembly lines. Meticulously stored, one above the other, as if we were on the way to school with Batman lunch boxes, a mother's love remained the same, despite the fact that her sons were all grown up. The lunch boxes were now rusted, and the school was now the brick and mortar of life's experiences—successes and failures.

My mother once told me that the best prayer I could pray, besides "Thy will be done," was for wisdom, knowledge, and understanding. Solomon asked for wisdom and not only was he wise, but he also lived abundantly. Years later, during my own struggles, I had questions that could not be answered from books alone or from the pulpit, for that matter. I needed answers—to build on, to give meaning to, and to learn from, not like a student who memorized only to forget later, but as one truly seeking answers to the puzzles of life.

Little did I suspect when I got the life-changing phone call from my big brother, Jim, that we would begin an odyssey that would be the impetus behind my "knowing." This journey propelled me to explore all of the "nooks and crannies" of my life that got me to this point. It was then that I had to decide if I was better off knowing or better off being blind.

* * *

Jim pulled up as I was putting my truck in the garage. I greeted him as we walked in the side door. Mom was in the kitchen, a place so full of memories, where we had seen her so many times.

"Hey, Mom," Jim said. "Are you sure you don't want to go?"

"Yeah. You all go. I have to keep the baby this weekend anyway. Give Linda and her sister a hug and tell them it's from me." Mom sounded adamant.

She would have liked to make the trip, but it was too rigorous to go and come right back in three days. She did not want to get stiff from the ride there and back.

"I sure will. They will probably be surprised to see us since Dad is already there," I said.

"Love ya, Mom—call you when we get there."

It seemed that as much as I wanted her to go, I did not want to see her sad. The memories of going home to the South were bittersweet, especially for my mother. It seemed that when you reached a certain point in life, you know more people on the "other side" than this one. I was determined to never let her experience the loneliness felt by the "last survivor."

Jim and I kissed Mom, said goodbye, and were on our way, already behind our self-imposed schedule. It was 1:00 p.m., and we were just leaving the city limits of Detroit on the way to Toledo. The pothole-ridden freeway was dotted with truckers, commuters, and recreational vehicles.

As we nestled into the plush tan leather interior of Jim's sport luxury sedan, we talked about old times, pulled out turkey sandwiches, and drank a Mountain Dew. Jim is what I call a successful, established man who played the game well. Married for twelve years with a wonderful wife and two gorgeous kids, Brit and Corbin, Jim appeared to be a template for corporate success.

He represented his company at college job fairs and was instrumental in the recruiting process. Knowing when to leave a dead end job for other opportunities was probably the key to Jim's success. Some called this "springboarding" when you looked ahead of the controlling, manipulative tactics of some employers who may see an employee as threatening if he or she attempted to progress beyond the cubicle.

Few employers want to hear that your focus is beyond their prescribed limitations, and when they do, you better be ready to make your move. Jim knew too well that, as a black man, you often fell prey to stigma, and your successes were often overshadowed by it. They ignored Jim's value for so long, he began looking for a new job. Like a symphony, this move must be well planned. It was so funny when Jim's old employer in beverage sales found out he was leaving. His last words were, "This is your last chance, if you want to come back." It's a good thing he moved on and risked possible termination.

I know this road so well, because I traveled it so many times—the highway, I-75 that was cut out from the industrial, now technological North, to and through the bluegrass state of Kentucky, and the Appalachian mountains of Tennessee. Jim lived and went to college in Tennessee. To him, these were no new sights. Living in Atlanta for nine years myself, I once viewed these states as only time and space 'till I got to my destination. Being a passenger, rather than a driver, gave me time to think of my experiences in the South.

Once viewed as the pathway to freedom and opportunity, my parents took this same road forty-five years ago, in hope of a better life for themselves and their children. Ironically, here we were on that same road headed south, while they ventured north.

We were almost in Dayton when it was time to get gas. We pulled over into a well-stocked, rural service station for some Mountain Dews, junk food, and gasoline. I took care of paying for the first fill-up while Jim stood under the awning, pumping gas in the rain. I browsed the store, not really knowing what I wanted, told the clerk to fill-up, then brought chips, a snack cake, and sodas to the counter. All the while, I felt the male clerk's eyes on me. It must have been my Persian lamb "Dr. Seuss-like" top hat.

"I must have made some mistake. I can't add the gas onto the food," the clerk called to the male doing stock. He quickly came and fixed the problem. She apologized, said it was her first day, and gave me back my change of eleven dollars. She miscounted and gave me ten dollars too much without knowing, because I spent nineteen dollars, and she should have given me only one back. I walked to the bathroom to count and just make sure, went out to where Jim was, and told him to pull closer out of the rain.

"Jim, this lady just gave me ten dollars too much, and it is her first day," I said.

"Give it back. We don't need their money."

"I was gonna'. I just didn't want to embarrass her."

There have been times when I would have and did take money when people made this type of mistake, but this time it was different. I did not want to see this lady lose her job due to her own incompetence, especially after being so polite. In this rural town, there was probably no place to work for ten miles if she was unemployed. Besides, we had much too great a journey ahead to gamble being dishonest. I waited until the male clerk was too far away to hear what was going on.

When I entered the station, three men who I could have mistaken for truckers looked on as I gave back the lady ten dollars and told her why. Perhaps we dispelled a myth.

In ancient times, and often today, a man's or woman's talents held the same value as money itself. A carpenter could always draw on his gift to build, thus support himself and his family. A talent, as described in the Bible, is a gift that is nurtured and developed to the fullest because it could be taken away if we bury it. Blessed is he who has many talents. When these talents amount to opportunities and earnings, it is time to ride the tide.

Even while being employed with a large corporation, I was always on the inside looking out and often running my own business without their knowledge. I always knew I could challenge myself to provide an excellent product if my talent was truly a gift. When I looked at my employers, they were no more intelligent, compassionate, or determined than I was. In fact, most lacked the moral qualities to be in control of so many people's lives. Nonetheless, I felt like a drop of water in the tide my employers rode on someone else's drive and creativity. I felt like a slave with options.

Since I lost my job as a sales supervisor for a major beverage distributor in 1992, I lost interest in working in an environment where I had little control. I had been fairly successful running two small businesses that had little in common except drive and creativity. During downtimes, I worked for people who ran their own small businesses—often friends and associates that had positions to fill. I knew firsthand that a business didn't have to be large to succeed—just have the right idea.

The glass ceiling and lack of control were probably my greatest complaints about some experiences in corporate employment. Something dawned on me one day as I was grinding out the Detroit area, preparing for an "important" corporate audit. As if a light bulb appeared over my head, that something said, *You are good enough to work like this for yourself. You are good enough.*

Although my businesses were small, they had great potential, and I have talked myself into major contracts, challenges, and opportunities. Most importantly, I gave a few people, not many, a chance to pay their bills, while also gaining a sense of confidence, accomplishment, and empowerment after a day's work. This is something I did not feel working for my last major employer. What I felt was rather powerlessness. This powerlessness turned into a "them versus us" attitude.

In my situation, I was given more and more accounts to keep me busy all the time. Yet, I would overhear some people say they were going home for lunch and to watch 'The Price Is Right' everyday, while I barely had time to make a phone call. This "them versus us" attitude intensified when my employer just happened to be white, and I realized that this guy who watches 'The Price Is Right' everyday—during work—happens to be a "valued" employee. He also happens to be white and makes two hundred dollars more a week than me, despite him having only a high school education. This amounts to eight hundred dollars a month more—a mortgage, car, what have you!

Someone once told me that if you are black, you must be better and work harder than your white counterparts to keep pace with corporate America. This could be difficult because many people in these positions are actually the best choices, although not all of them. I was privileged to attend a training seminar for the fastest growing cellular phone company, Nextel. The gentleman who led the training had jumped ship from Dale Carnegie; he was borderline brilliant. The fact that he was white did not matter much to me. Certainly he could have been given more opportunity to get to this point, but in his mid-fifties, he had arrived. I think of what Thomas Jefferson said in his "Notes on the State of Virginia" message about the colonists. His point was that "one improvement begets another," ultimately increasing the chances for improvement. Someone, somewhere opened the door. It happens all the time.

First of all, you must be considered "safe" to get in the door, attuned with the white corporate culture while, in some cases, downplaying your own. Get one thing straight; there is no black corporate culture. (If you believe so, try wearing a dashiki to your next board meeting.) But seriously, take a look at the busy New York Financial District as people spill out during lunchtime. Look for a mustache, beard, or goatee in this sea of people. You will see few, and the few that you see, especially beards, belong to established executives and foreigners. This environment does not allow newcomers to successfully set their own standards or buck any trends, unless they are a computer guru in Silicone Valley. Although some companies are more relaxed today, the culture still applies.

To be considered "safe," you must comply with the dress and psyche of your corporate provider, with constant assurance that your views are the same. For blacks, this seems to be an even greater task, since compliance only rehashes a historical eyesore and reinforces old stereotypes. I question the effect that this institutionalized giant has on controlling one's psyche, limiting one's creativity, and perpetuating the great racial divide. Reliance leading to fear of stability and security comes when the corporate ladder's progress is interrupted for whatever reason. When the economy catches a cold, minorities always seem to catch the flu. Call it the nature of the beast.

Chapter 2

Le Cygne Restaurant, Ramada Renaissance Hotel, Atlanta, Georgia 1986. A harpist strummed the sweet melody of a classical tune, perhaps Bach or Beethoven, while guests dined and talked in the elegant, candlelit setting of one of Atlanta's top gourmet restaurants. Le Cygne (French for 'The Swan') was located a short shuttle ride from Atlanta's Hartsfield International Airport. In contrast to the heavenly serenity of the dining room, all hell broke loose in the kitchen, which could be mistaken for the airport's main runway itself. Executive chefs screamed at sous chefs, while bartenders scurried to complete drink orders for tuxedo-clad waiters. The cashier was ringing overtime, tallying up the busy restaurant's revenue. The specials of the day were Norwegian Turbot, Chicken Oscar, and Foie Gras (goose liver pate) in a puff pastry shell with a red wine sauce for an appetizer, and Sabayon, over raspberries, prepared tableside for dessert.

As the front waiter, I handled the guests, tableside service, drinks, and bill, which brought me to the area between the service bar and cashier, which was getting backed up and starting to look like a penguin welfare line. Seeing the congestion in the back service area and knowing that guests were still being seated, I started to sweat; my bow tie clung tightly around the winged-tip shirt of my neck. The bartender was busy to my left and the cashier was busy to my right, although I needed them both right away and didn't have time to wait for either. Just seconds before I darted to the dining room to greet the new guests and deal with the "L.A. traffic jam" later, Jim Reed walked in red-faced and angry. Suddenly, behind the soundproof door that separated the noisy kitchen from the serene dining area, a much greater noise and chaos broke loose. It was Jim Reed's voice reacting to the delay.

"Kirk, you are nothing but a worthless piece of shit!" he shouted.

The kitchen and service area went silent; the cooks, bartenders, cashier, and waiters stopped what they were doing at that time. It was as if Jim Reed and I were onstage, and everyone there was the audience. My pride was at stake; I could have easily solved this with a right cross and left uppercut ... but I didn't. It would not have been professional.

Kirk Coleman

I stood there in a trance for seconds, which seemed like minutes, slowly turned to my right, and looked him straight in his eyes as we fronted off like two male lions fighting for mating rights. I squinted and looked into him so deeply, past the whites, the corneas, through the pupils, and ultimately to his soul, trying to make sense of what he just said to me. When I finally reached the depths of his total being, through eye contact, where we were just men without the protection of class or title, he turned and walked away.

I didn't want to risk a one hundred eighty dollar a night gig by exploding and crashing this silver spoon-fed idiot's grill—although I came close. I learned early that I must control the outcome of my situation, because it was my very, very own. Why did some people push me to the limits of what I would take or let them get away with? Why did they, too often, try to set me up for failure, thinking they could predict my actions, my demise, like a one-sided, one-dimensional character of a minstrel show? I always believed that if my foes could not predict, or anticipate my actions, they could never beat me. What I had in store for Jim Reed was something he would have never expected.

Just why would this man try to convince me that I was a "worthless piece of shit" one week after the restaurant received a letter from international business travelers, exclusively commending my service? They added that, when they came to Atlanta, our restaurant would be the "first place they come to for dinner." What was it that would make Jim Reed say this? I searched and searched for some explanation.

Could it be the internship I was awarded over one hundred fifty applicants with the <u>Atlanta Journal Constitution</u> newspaper? Could it be my determination to keep both jobs that summer of 1986? Could it be my new, high-performance motorcycle or my old classical BMW? My motorcycle was vandalized in the hotel employee parking lot. Could it be that instead of going out for drinks with Jim, I always went home to study for an English degree?

My curious mind, fresh with the ideologies of Cullen, Keats, Shelley, and McKay (especially McKay), took me to deeper thoughts, thoughts which led to anger. The crisp Atlanta air gave me a short-term sense of freedom as I tucked my head, tightened my legs, and cut and sliced my way home at speeds pressing 100 mph down I-75 North. When I got to my exit, I-20 west, I was breathing heavily, adrenaline pumping through my veins, my temples throbbing.

Maybe I should have punched him. If he used the "N" word, I might have killed him right there or killed myself on the way home. *Next time*, I thought, *the spa would be a much safer place to blow off steam.*

When I woke up the next morning, I was at peace with the situation that ruined my night. Within the course of the night, a simple prescription for validation of all claims came to mind in three simple words—*"Consider the source."*

Just who was this man, so power hungry, that he had his head and foot up Mr. Johansen's ass at the same time? (Mr. Johansen was the Danish maitre d' from Copenhagen.) Until his remark, we never had any problems because we had something in common. We were both from Michigan; although he was from Grosse Point, a wealthy suburb, he claimed my hometown, Detroit. From a well-to-do banking family, he could have had anything; but he was a self-proclaimed alcoholic who was kicked out of Michigan State University and temporarily shut out of the family fortune as punishment. He drained Mr. Johansen of all that it took to run the restaurant and stabbed him in the back when my two-page typed complaint hit human resources three days later. Did you think it wouldn't?

Later that week, Jim and I were called to human resources to address my complaint. The stone-faced personnel director fired off a series of questions. Jim Reed was now in the hot seat, clinching his hands and turning red.

"Did you call Mr. Coleman 'a worthless piece of shit'?" she asked.

"I may have said something like that. We were in the middle of a rush, and Kirk was in the weeds—if I remember correctly."

I looked at him, then looked off, staring at the ceiling. *Couldn't remember calling someone "a worthless piece of shit,"* I thought.

"Look at this letter," she said, producing the letter of commendation. He read the letter. "Don't you think Mr. Coleman, or anybody, deserves better than to be called 'a worthless piece of shit'?"

"You don't understand," he said nervously. "We were in a rush, and it was not all my doing. Mr. Johansen told me to say ... told me to ... um ... to put pressure on Kirk."

"Did Mr. Johansen tell you to call Mr. Coleman 'a worthless piece of shit'?"

"No ... no, he didn't."

"But you did."

"He told me to put some pressure on him. He thought Kirk could do a better job."

Ah-ha. Mr. Johansen told Jim to provoke me, and I wondered if the letter had anything to do with it. There were also other things that puzzled me. I was the front waiter in a profession where blacks were often satisfied with the rear. Somehow, I felt my job would have been easier if I hadn't taken on the challenges of the front waiter. I was articulate, good with guests, and fluent with the French menu, so I thought I deserved it. I always wondered if they felt differently.

Mr. Johansen told Jim to provoke me, and Jim did what he was told. They were drinking buddies. After an investigation, Mr. Johansen was forced to resign three weeks later, and to my astonishment, Jim took his job as maitre d'. Knowing that I could not learn from Jim, and he was ultimately rewarded for what he did, I turned in my two-week resignation shortly after he assumed his position. He continued to progress in hotel management because he played the game well and was somewhat handsome and shrewd, as required in this industry. He eventually left Le Cygne after more drinking-related controversy.

Last I heard, Jim worked at the Ritz Carlton as restaurant manager, while I moved on to the signature restaurant, J. W's, in the new Marriott Marquis while supervising banquets at the convention center. I regretted that Mr. Johansen lost his job, but I needed to find out why this incident took place. They had tried to set me up. When people rubbed me the wrong way, I needed answers. Somehow I just couldn't let things go. To this day, I have yet to find if this behavior of mine is a blessing or a curse.

Six hours after we started out on our trip, my brother and I were entering the state of Kentucky. The rain was starting to clear. Like a child, I was looking at the sky, trying to make sense of cloud formations. Like an adult, I was looking for any message heaven might send, but I knew it really wasn't that simple. As the warm sun appeared through the mountainous clouds, the sunroof opened, and we were closer to nature. We began to recount some of our experiences.

"Do you remember when we walked in Club Leumo and didn't know it was gay night?" Jim gave a hearty laugh, his eyes twinkling from the memory.

"How could I forget?" I chuckled.

When I left for college two years before, this club was somewhat straight, but it wasn't this night. Amidst the smoke and haze, we must have been there a good two minutes without noticing anything different. We could only see the frantic movement allowed by a strobe light and, I might add, some pretty good dance moves. The women we found in the club were, of course, dancing with each other and the men appeared to be having the time of their lives.

Although somewhat comfortable with homosexuals from Atlanta's hotel industry, I was not expecting this. (The best waiters in the best restaurants, for some reason, were usually gay. They just floated across the room, were articulate, and had a personality like no other.) We, however, were looking for women and agreed that we should leave before we saw someone we knew. As we were walking towards the exit, that's *exactly* what happened. I saw someone I knew.

I grew up faster because of Jim, who was one-and-a-half years older than I. There were things he could not do because he was not old enough that I did at the same age. Because of our close age, I followed him when he got his freedom. I went to parties and concerts with him, from Pat Metheney to Parliament/Funkadelic, at an age he could not. As a child, he was given direct orders when I was born to watch over me because I was clumsy, curious, got stuck behind couches, and fought to use my left hand. He became familiar with being a father long before he had his own kids. He was like a father to DeMal, our younger brother. Not mistaken for a saint, however, Jim was the architect of some major capers that we still don't talk about to this day. He just tends to forget as he relaxes into his world of polo green, golf clubs, expensive cigars, and "hob-nobbery." I'm proud of him though.

I saw my mother in his face. The nose, long in length, was just like hers. The face, glowing and trusting, won friends and allegiances easily. Besides a stillborn—also a boy—Jim was the first of three boys born to James and Ludeal Coleman in the early stages of their marriage. They were young, ambitious, faithful, and probably deeply in love at that time, and their well-adjusted seed was a result of that bond. DeMal and I, however, came at different stages of their marriage. As the Bible simply states, "You reap what you sow."

Jim was getting tired and pulled into a service station to get gas a few miles outside of Munfreesboro, Tennessee. When he came out of the station, he went to the passenger's side with an auto classified magazine. He said, "Wanna drive?" I figured it was about time. I knew Jim did not like to drive through Munfreesboro because he got a ticket going eighty-five miles an hour when the family went down South over twenty years ago that he *still* has not paid. Dad was not with us.

"Okay, no problem," I said.

I ascribed to a certain etiquette when riding on trips with people who drove their own car that I applied to other situations as well. I always waited until they asked me to drive, and they always did if the trip was long enough. I recalled my first trip to Atlanta with my first roommate, Marzell. We had a trailer on the back of my car, and we took along Al, his cousin. I was not really clear on Al's motivation for going to Atlanta, but I *did* know that he was too old for college, and he brought almost everything he had in three packages.

"Just let me know when you get tired, man," Al had said in a raspy voice. "I even brought my driving gloves."

"Alright, man," I said, but wondered if he had a car or even drove one recently.

I let Marzell drive when I got tired, then I took the wheel later. Al still kept asking to put his Italian racing gloves to use. (It was, by now, what I imagined the gloves to be.) Needless to say, I never let him drive. When we got to Atlanta, he was angry and somewhat defeated. It must have been the driving gloves. If I learned nothing else from Al, I learned this much. Even Ella Fitzgerald sang: "God Bless the Child That's Got His Own ... That's Got His Own."

As I took control of the sports sedan like it was my own, Jim reclined in the passenger seat to look at what Tennessee had to offer for vintage cars. This is what we talked about most. Jim and I were always humorously comparing our two cars, his '66 Mustang and my black '68 Lincoln Continental. I would refer to Jim's driveway as the Mustang graveyard because he had two, and his '66 never ran much since he came back from Tennessee. He, however, didn't let me forget the time I was driving and my car caught fire. I took off my jacket and tried to put the fire out with it.

Unfortunately, it turned out to be a flammable jacket, so I burned my hands, somewhat seriously, as the flames crept up the back firewall, gaining strength with each hose and wire conquered. Defeated, I gave up, checked for valuables and realized that my car was toast. Through the smoke I could see this white guy in a shirt and tie running frantically across the street with a fire extinguisher.

"Pull the plug and spray," he said.

He gave me the extinguisher, and I quickly put the fire out. I thanked him and thanked God for him. Then I got back into the car, turned the key, and the car started! After arriving at my destination, I left the car there until later, wondering if it was possessed.

By this time, we had logged two-thirds of our destination and had talked about many things. Approaching the state of Alabama from Tennessee, the roads changed in color to a reddish hue that I recognized. Jim woke up after about an hour and a half sleep, at ease with my driving ability. This time nobody talked. I wondered if he was thinking what I was thinking. If he was not, we were not being fair in our purpose of taking the trip in the first place. Maybe it was avoidance. We often avoided a topic that made us sad, I thought. Sad or not, I felt we were cheating DeMal and ourselves by ignoring the facts. Maybe Jim was thinking the same thing I was. *It was time*, I thought.

"Have you been to the graveside since they put the headstone down?"

"No, not yet."

When the dead are buried, the ground must settle for six months before a headstone could be planted. Until it did, the only markings you had were numbers on the bare soil or other gravesides. Then I spoke in the childish, hotheaded tone that I was known for before learning diplomacy.

"I'm not trying to forget that this or he ever happened."

Turning away from the window, Jim looked at me. "DeMal spent more time with me than anybody. He talked to my wife the day this happened and once told me if anything happened to him, he wanted me to take care of his son. He was like my son."

It was then that I realized that both of us had gone through the same experience, and our losses were the same. I relented, not wanting to talk or think about this again soon.

I love Chicago. The women are divine, and everyone is beautiful, trendy, and cosmopolitan. By the same token, the city is cold and callous, where police wear bulletproof vests on the outside, and the weather helps control the crime rate. A city of intrigue, I try to visit Chicago twice a year when I can because Chicago, to me, is just like home.

My parents once lived in Chicago, right across from Ogden Park, right on 64th and Loomis. The two-family brownstone, after sandblasting, remained virtually the same today as it was in 1960. Sadly, the people in this picture changed dramatically, weathered in the course of time. My uncle Seright, Mom's oldest and only living brother, is in a wheelchair under constant hospitalization. His wife, aunt Bet, is in her mid-eighties and struggles to perform everyday tasks.

At one point, this house was so full of life—old and new. Jim, or James Coleman Jr., was a newborn. My uncle was janitor at a local school. Mom kept house and kept everyone fed, while Dad sought a niche in Chicago's job market at a bakery. I was there, tucked away in the safety of my mother's womb, but I—*was*—*there* when my father stumbled into the underworld of Chicago's nightlife.

I can only speculate when this whole thing began, but all I know is Chicago is when and where it was discovered. Sometime before, during, or after my conception, Dad, God bless him, discovered his gift. The alcohol was no secret, but this one was. Since you usually get away with your secret activity the first time, he was no rookie when his secret was revealed, to his embarrassment.

Somewhere in the course of his marriage, he discovered that the same smooth, convincing language that he used to woo, catch, and marry my mother worked on other women as well. The smooth operator was born at the expense of the family. It was as if the airport I landed in had only one person in the control tower, because my dad, at the time, appeared to be sowing his wild oats. Love, faithfulness, and commitment were changing to deception; but a strong, determined woman helped keep things together for a while.

It was about 2:30 one cold Chicago morning when my mother was awakened by four taps on her bedroom window. It was Dad, who had somehow squeezed between the brownstones trying not to draw any attention.

"Lu, open the back door," he whispered. When she looked out and saw what appeared to be his face, she was overtaken with tremendous fear. She ran down the hallway and opened the door. My father stumbled in, dazed and bloodied.

"What happened—who did this to you?" Mother gasped.

"I was at a bar and two guys jumped on me," he murmured through his swollen, blood-soaked lips.

"Seright!" she shouted.

"No, no," he said, trying to be discreet.

With two eyes bruised and closed, looking like the aftermath of a fight scene from Rocky II, there was no way to hide. His secret was soon revealed. Nevertheless, Mom took care of him like her child until he fully recovered.

After my uncle Seright investigated, we found this to be no random act of violence. It turned out that these men just happened to know whose ass they kicked, and why they did it. Two notorious hoodlums, who were brothers, crossed paths this night with my father in a bar. Their sister was also there. Need I say more? I will. Boy meets girl. Boy likes girl. Boy really, really likes girl. Boy says something nasty to girl.

Girl's brothers don't like boy. Girl's brothers kick boy's ass.

This night Dad was beaten unconscious and left for dead on the cold sidewalk. The two men actually didn't know if they killed him or not as he lay motionless outside the bar. A passing motorist stopped, revived him, and brought him home. It was then that my destiny changed. My family decided to leave Chicago and move back to Detroit. If I told anyone that I was one ass kicking from being from Chicago, they would think I was crazy. By just a few months, I missed being born in the city I loved.

Night was falling on our journey, and Jim was back at the wheel of the Polo green Acura. We were nearing the place where our parents met and married, the place where we had spent weeks every summer vacation growing up. This was the place where, over thirty years ago, kids would gather around and listen to Jim and I talk, as if we were from another country. The place where, sadly, to this day, you could still be called a "watermelon-eatin' coon," and still not respond.

Alabama, with its underlying and historical current of fear and aggression, lacked the complexities of large Northern cities. It was not cosmopolitan, like Chicago, Atlanta, and New York, where the races, at least, came together as one for the purpose of survival. The only boundary you might find could be camouflaged as opportunity. Alabama is simply Alabama. You have railroad tracks, and you know what's on either side.

Out of my large family in the South, I did not know anyone over sixty that hadn't experienced the fear of Alabama. T. K. Lampkin, a sharecropper in Fort Deposit, Alabama, one day decided that rations of food and a place to stay were not enough for his growing family. His work ethic made him a valuable employee to the landowners of the post-slavery era of the early 1930s. They still needed bodies to maintain an operation started years ago or face poverty.

When it was revealed that he wanted out, fear was used to keep him in place, and this fear was for his life. His captors, or employers, could not see him progressing beyond their needs, so he had to make his move or die. One day, before sunrise, he left town hidden in a horse-drawn wagon, covered with hay, to begin a new life. This was not a grand exit, but considering the time and place, a wise one. His wife, Amy Smith, gave birth to six children before dying in her mid-thirties of a kidney ailment. She was buried in Fort Deposit. His sister, who had already moved to Chicago, died in a house fire, so he took on and raised her child, Mitt, in addition to Seright, Lola, Inez, Ludeal, Mattie, and Joel, his own six.

My grandfather, T. K. Lampkin, thank God for his genes, was a strict, strong, disciplinary man who taught his boys to be men and his girls to be women. The tall, handsome, dark brown-skinned man worked at U.S. Steel and provided his family every opportunity to grow. He, being a single parent who never remarried, also faced monumental challenges.

The little girl Ludeal who lost her mother at age four, cried all the time. A strong father figure could not make up for her loss; she was still traumatized growing up without a mother. She often wondered what it would be like with a mother, what a mother would do, and how her life would be different. This void produced a great deal of energy that could be satisfied only in the course of achievement. She joined the church at an early age and excelled in school, passing her older brothers and sisters, and eventually graduated at the top of her class. All the while she worked for Reverend Holmes, her pastor, cooking and doing accounting for the church. Her motivation to fill this void led her younger sister and brother, Matt and Joel, to church as well. She walked three miles each day to attend Miles College, where she graduated in three years.

    This miraculously determined child, I am proud to say, is my mother. Long, raven-black hair, nice hips, slim waist, and strong Indian features from her mother made her the object of many men's affection. But who would she choose to accompany her in life's most important and challenging stage?

Chapter 3

Almost clearing the mountains of Tennessee and nearing the Alabama border, I thought of my experiences in "Sweet Home Alabama," although it was not my home. It was my home away from home and once my parents' home. Nonetheless, I still felt connected because of my experiences there. I remembered Lola's house and the old house where my grandfather lived, and that was what came to mind most when I thought of the South. The old house has gone, faded away into the industrial landscape of the railroad tracks that ran behind it. Like it was yesterday, I remember the oil heater and the screened-in front porch. I remember the chicken-coop in the backyard where I got the name "Chicken Hawk" as though it were only yesterday.

Although my Dad had family in the South and we visited them as well, this area was where we spent most of our summers. This was as much a part of my heritage as the North. As I grew older, however, I knew I did not want to live in Alabama for the same reason many people left there in the first place. I could not understand the undercurrent of fear that these people were controlled by, although the control was honest in form.

Before I left Detroit, I telephoned my cousin, Dave Moorer, in Atlanta. He was one of my favorite cousins; he commanded the respect of all of my uncles, but, nonetheless, was a cousin. Being my father's first cousin on my grandfather's side made him my second cousin, although he seemed closer.

Dave, an IBM executive who went to Morehouse, let me stay with him when I first came down for college. He married his college sweetheart, Betty, and by now had two college-age children. The last time I saw him was at a family reunion in Stone Mountain, Georgia. No, it was a funeral, but I didn't remember very much then. However, when I saw him, I gave him a picture of Chyna and me that said, "Aloha from Hawaii."

"Kirk, do you remember the 'gourmet-for-two' concept you started years ago in Atlanta?" he asked.

When I first started catering in Atlanta in 1987, I experimented with this concept, but with limited success. I provided items such as Stuffed Trout in a

Honey-Lemon Sauce and Crusted Rack of Lamb with a Mandarin Glaze for two, over Snow Peas, with wine, disposable glasses, and candlelight for the tune of one hundred dollars.

"Yeah."

"Man, they took that idea and ran with it!"

"Oh yeah, wow! What, some white boys?"

"Yeah. When I saw that on TV, I immediately thought of you, man. You are way ahead of your time."

"Ten years, aye."

"Have you tried that in Detroit?"

"Yeah, but it's only seasonal here, like Valentine's Day or Sweetest Day. Large-volume catering is where the business is right now," I added.

"Do you still have a food service contract with the museum?"

"No. After a year and a half, we terminated it, but we are still honoring parties booked beforehand, which are quite a few."

"Why did the contract get terminated?" he asked. Then I thought, *Boy! This man asks a lot of questions.*

"Bullshit and money. Too much bullshit and too little money."

"Isn't that The Museum of African-American History?" he asked.

"Yeah."

"Isn't it run by blacks?"

"Yeah."

Perplexed, he asked, "So what's the problem?"

"Cuz, I think you already answered the question."

"Enough said, Cuz. I'm ready to come up there for a wedding. When are you gonna' tie the knot with Chyna?"

Then I thought of how much he used to love Lena when I lived in Atlanta. He only met two, Lena and Chyna, but he fell in love with them both. I wondered if he just wanted to see me married to someone, feeling then my life would be complete. He said he liked the girls I picked, their qualities and all. Although I've yet to marry, every girl he met, he said, would make a good wife.

"I know you're not gonna take just anybody to Hawaii. Is she the one?"

"Yeah, man, she's the one."

His curiosity was beginning to annoy me. "When?"

"Soon, real soon. When I took this contract, I turned down two job offers with two large companies, Nabisco and Ameritech, so I'm somewhat transitional at this point. Either I pursue another contract and work myself like a dog or go back into the job market, possibly with the State. I'm too risky for some women," I exclaimed.

"That's what business is about—risk," he asserted.

"Yeah, it is."

Anyone who has spent any time pursuing a dream knows that the dream is sometimes better off on the horizon because reality, for some reason, dulls the senses. Anyone privileged to live their dream could also sleepwalk through it if they didn't pay close attention or they could wake up to a nightmare. I spent a great deal of time and energy securing a major food service contract, only to find that it took a toll on my mind, body, relationships, and spirit. This, the pinnacle of my catering career, marked the turning point as well. Sometimes dreams were larger than life, but this one was lived and life went on. Nothing of a tangible or material nature lasted forever.

Although a red oak and a rosebush flourished differently, who is to say which was better? Being a rosebush in the winter wasn't so bad with the hope of spring.

Chapter 4

My brother and I were clearing the state of Tennessee while the sun was sinking behind the hills. Sunlight had given way to twilight; stars were lined up, taking their places for a spectacular nighttime display. I thought about all the places I was privileged to go or live at and wondered why the stars in the sky remained the same, regardless where I traveled. With those thoughts, I relished the starlit night until I drifted off somewhere between sleep and consciousness, while thinking of the life I left behind in Detroit.

* * *

When I think about it, the mayor, celebrities, and dignitaries from all over the world attended parties that were catered in the new museum under my care. When it first opened, everyone wanted to have a party or be seen there. I was privileged to be there myself and owed it to the trust and generosity of people like Stephanie Clark, director of marketing, who was confident in my abilities and supported my blue prints for success, while others felt I was just a fast-talking slickster trying to "hit a lick."

Once in, I hit the ground running, living up to my commitment to make the museum a world-class act in catering, while implementing a box lunch program for schoolchildren. I had a vision, and although some people tried to hijack it and shape it as their own, my plan was written almost a year before and was sitting on Stephanie's and the director's desks. Everyone had a better idea, it seemed, and tested my laid-back management approach. Some people got their feelings hurt.

I somehow knew I wouldn't be there forever, so I decided to make the best of it and have a little fun at the same time. I spent almost two years planning to be where I was today, and I didn't want it to pass by without notice. This was my dream, and I wanted to savor the opportunity. I checked the kitchen, waltzed the rotunda, mingled with and scoped out the ladies, directed the tuxedoed waiters, and picked up a large check from the client (although there was much more to it than that). I was getting paid doing what I loved to do. I was a rose in early spring.

Kirk Coleman

This is for me, I thought. *I am living my dream.*

At the time, Mom must have thought I was crazy for delaying two corporate job offers in one week, but she knew how much I wanted this food service contractor position. I got tired of waiting for this thing to go through—contract and all. I was about to take one of the two jobs until something happened. On Friday, at 4:00 p.m., I got this call from Wayne, the director of facilities at the museum, who put me under much unneeded pressure from the start.

"Hi, Kirk. This is Wayne."

"Hey, Wayne."

"I would like you to open the restaurant Monday," he said.

"Oh yeah, today is Friday—that might be difficult," I responded.

"Kirk, do you know Chef Lenn?"

"Yeah. I've heard of him."

"I tell you what, Kirk. Go meet Chef Lenn and see if you guys can work together. If you can, we'll do a three-way split on the restaurant revenue. I'll have a temporary contract written up, if you guys can work together."

"Okay; see you Monday," I said.

Then I wondered, *Was he talking about gross or net?*

Let me think. I had Ameritech expecting me for a four-day training session in Ohio, Nabisco's job offer in hand (but it didn't pay enough), and the museum work started Monday. It was like I had come to the end of a *road that split up three ways. Each was identical with no highs or lows, and of course, no signs or directions.*

"Pray over it," Mother said.

I did, but not on my knees. Monday morning I chose my own business over someone else's by walking through the doors of the world's largest African-American museum to begin a food service contract. Although I was not a gambler, maybe it was a risk. Maybe it was just my need to be in control of my own destiny. For the life of me, I have yet to find if this was a blessing or a curse.

We set the standard for the new museum, and the standard was high. Doing three parties a day, plus a restaurant, was a common day's work. We became so busy, that I had to rent an apartment three blocks away to regroup. Of course Chyna did not like the idea. She said I could be saving that money for other uses—the future and the like. But getting off sometimes at 1:00 a.m. and being back at 5:00 a.m. left me no choice.

In retrospect, Chyna was right because the apartment had duel uses—business and pleasure. After some parties, I would drink champagne and flirt with my favorite waitresses. I needed to unwind though. It got to the point where somebody would look up and ask, "Where is Kirk?" They would look out in the lot for my truck or van, and it would be gone. Sometimes I would pick Chyna up, take her to the movie, and sometimes fall asleep before it ended. I was married to the occupation that I worked so hard for; there was nothing else I could do. I could accept personal failure, but not here and not now. Little did I know that the greatest work was ahead of me, perhaps of my entire life. Failure happened, but this was my dream, although it was not always pleasant. Satisfying the masses was not easy. There were people there who did not like me and thought I was overpaid. I was okay with that. What puzzled and disappointed me the most was that despite my numerous race-related experiences of the past, these were people just like me.

* * *

Although almost three years have passed, I remember the day so clearly as if it were yesterday. I left home about 9:30 that Friday morning and noticed what an unusually gorgeous day it was for September. The sun seemed to shine brighter than normal. There was no haze, no extreme heat, no cold, just a picturesque, perfect day.

It could never rain, I thought. The only clouds in the sky were white, sparse, and friendly. This was good because, in addition to a sit-down, four-course meal which included soup—we didn't have soup bowls yet—I had a buffet and art gallery outside, under a tent for two hundred people.

A busy, hectic day could not have started out any better than this, however. I needed twelve waiters, so I called Laura and Paris, my best waiters, on the cell phone. Laura was one of five people I employed who were white. Even though I often got some flack about this, I thought hiring people of different cultures gave the museum a universal flair. I used Laura before I even got to the museum though. She was loyal, pretty, smart, and I liked her a lot. One New Year's Eve, we had a party and had to work most of the night. When midnight came around, and people hugged, kissed, and celebrated the New Year, I pulled her closer and we kissed, hugged, and toasted in the New Year, as well.

I had no problems hiring people who were gay or somewhat eccentric because I have been mistaken for both. As an employer, I did not discriminate; instead, I went out of my way to motivate people through empowerment and reward, not fear. Jim, who watched the bottom line, told me I spent too much on labor and costs and everything else. Catering is just one business where you can't take shortcuts and still be successful. Good help and good food cost money.

On my way in that Friday morning, I planned my day from beginning to end. After the last party was served, I planned to get Chyna, go to the art fair at the university, come back and make sure the kitchen was closed, and spend some time with her. My busy, around-the-clock schedule had me in the doghouse, but I planned to use tonight to patch things up.

When I pulled in the parking lot, I waved to the guard on my way in. It was bright and clear. I saw the reflection of my van on the doorway's glass in radiant proportions (and I hadn't even washed it!). I waltzed in, speaking to everyone in the corridor, eager to take on the tasks at hand. I spoke to everybody as they performed their tasks. The cooks were finishing up breakfast and working on lunch for the restaurant. I looked on the board at the function sheets to see what needed to be done to prepare for this big night. It was almost surreal that the dishwashers were all there; no one called in; everything was going full steam ahead.

I made a list with my partner, Lenn, and the cook, Charlotte, then went to the market for needed supplies. He was expecting a baby from his wife—or one of his wives, to be exact. He had the convenience of both of them strategically placed on opposite sides of town. He knew it would be some time soon that his third child from this third woman was expected. Somehow, for some strange reason, I admired him though, because his kids were a product of his lifelong travels, although his choices in women were different from my own. *I could have at least had one of the babies that I created in Atlanta*, I thought. (I loved Lena differently than anyone I have met, and she loved me. She was so feisty. I didn't try hard enough to talk her out of the situation we encountered, and I have thought about it often. She had fears, and so did I.) Nonetheless, Lenn dogged his women. I have witnessed many profanity-laced arguments in the kitchen, office, and parking lot. To say he had middle-class women or acted that way himself would be an overstatement, but the man loved his kids and he could burn (cook).

SINZ OF THE FATHA

It was about 1:00 p.m. Friday when Lenn got the call. His wife, or woman (she would say he was her husband, but he never really acknowledged this to me, so I didn't know) was in labor. He was ecstatic. He wanted to immediately leave and go to the hospital, but knew we had too much to do prepping and serving two parties simultaneously by 5:00 p.m., while being in the middle of a busy lunch. I assured him that everything would be all right and told him to go see about his wife, girlfriend, or whatever. We discussed what needed to be done as I walked him down the long corridor, out to the parking lot, and patted him on his back, and wished him well. Outside it was still a beautiful day.

With Lenn gone, this left me solely responsible for what happened this evening. I was going to make sure everything was good. It was my day of total autonomy and control. Everything ran like clockwork; I was the engine that powered it. This is what I lived for. This is what I planned for. Forget yesterday. Forget tomorrow. Today was my day. This was why I chose my business over someone else's. I could not explain the satisfaction I felt not having to fight, or jockey for position. I wouldn't miss this day for the world, because everyday was not like this day.

Chef Lenn, my partner, although not by choice, was shrewd, cocky, and overbearing. His style of management and manner of treating people was different than my own. Needless to say, we clashed and had separate loyalties among staff. He once told me that I was "too nice" to be in this type of business; he may have been right. I changed in the course of time, having to fight just to keep order. The handpicked, polished, refined people I brought in were under constant siege by what I called pirates. It all came to a climax before one of the biggest sit-down parties in the history of the museum—five hundred people. The incident was all about power and control; I lost control. Chef Lenn and I whirled profanities at each other in front of the shocked kitchen staff, not backing down because of our "caterers' egos." As he walked out, I continued using words Donald Goines might think twice about.

While following him out the door, I continued my verbal assault. Because of the acoustics in the new facility, this argument reverberated out to one of the meeting rooms where, Deacon Carter, a prominent deacon in my church, was attending! I lamented, wondering what I was becoming and if all this was really worth it. On top of that, I was gaining weight due to the availability of food, and this was accompanied by extra stress. I had gone to college, earned a degree in English, and was using words not listed in any dictionary I could think of.

It was 3 p.m. The waiters were coming in to get their assignments as I decorated the outside tables with cloths of fine African prints, encircled by fresh white skirts. A busy lunch was wrapping up. I had about eight hundred dollars in my pocket from a previous drop at my restaurant. *Looked like a twelve hundred dollar day in the restaurant,* I computed. The sky was clear, perfect for an outside party.

Certainly nothing can go wrong today, I thought.

The dishwasher told me to pick up the phone; it was Lenn. He was still at the hospital. His wife (or whatever) was expected to deliver the baby any moment. He called to see if I located the soup bowls. I told him everything was taken care of.

"Go on, enjoy this day. I'm your partner, man. I've got you covered. Go on. Gotta go. See ya."

At 4:10 p.m., all the waiters were assigned and performing their duties. I could smell the food from the convection ovens as I was talking with Phil, my gofer guy. Then Sean Tiller, a bartender and friend who also ran his own business, arrived. I walked him out to the tent where his bar would be set up and noticed that the cloud cover was increasing. Returning to the dining room to do a check, my pager went off. It was Mother.

What could Mother want? I thought. She never calls me at work, even though I call her all the time.

I went to the kitchen phone to see what she wanted.

"Hey, Mom, what's going on?"

"Kirk, I need you to come home. DeMal had a seizure at work."

"What!? Mom, is he all right—I have two big parties star—"

"Kirk, please. I need you here now," her voice quivered.

Kirk Coleman

When I heard that quiver in her voice, I knew something was terribly wrong, and I had to go. I was hammered and numbed at the same time.

"Phil, I have to go—handle it," were my last words as I rushed out.

It was raining. I left the museum and didn't look back. Entering the freeway in route home, I drove like an ambulance driver in a life or death situation. Unlike my trip to work, I noticed nothing. Anything within my vanishing point appeared to be an obstacle in my way. I prayed all the way home that everything would be all right, but there was something about my mother's voice. Although I'm like my father in many ways, she and I were keenly mysteriously and spiritually linked. I could bring her something home, and she would say that's exactly what she had wanted. It was eerie and so was this.

I got off the freeway, running lights, somehow thinking I could manage or control this situation, but I knew I could not. This was in God's hands. When I pulled my van in the driveway, I saw DeMal's mother-in-law on the porch. She cut me off as I bolted to the door.

"Kirk, you have to be strong for your mother. DeMal is dead," she said.

I took off frantically, not wanting to hear this from anyone other than my mother, who I loved and knew loved me. When I saw her face as she sat in her lazy-boy rocker, I knew it was true, but still asked anyway.

"Is it true, Mom, is it?"

"Yes ... he died."

For a moment, my mouth flew open, no words coming out. Finally, I found my voice. "Oh, no—my baby brother; no!"

I grabbed Mother and cried in her arms for I don't know how long. I grieved and grieved and grieved and then went numb with acceptance, while welcoming any opportunity for denial. It was not just raining; it was storming. People started to pour into the house. I knew Mom had company, so I left.

I do not really know how and why I ended up back at the museum, but somehow I found myself there. I surveyed the remnants of the outside party, which was rained out, although Sean, professional as he was, manned the bar like the captain of a ship. When he heard about what happened, he gave me a hug and poured me an Absolut and cranberry that I sipped once and put down. Laura and Dawn found me and their hugs were welcomed as well. This time, however, I did not notice the softness, scent, or anything else that made a woman a woman. I saw Robert, the drinking bartender, one of Chef Lenn's guys. Although my adversary in much of my business dealings, his words were the kindest, his hug was the longest. He also told me that Lenn's wife had the baby around 3:30 p.m., about the same time my brother died. Today I saw Robert like never before. I opened up to him and gave him all the money in my pocket from the restaurant to hand over to Lenn, not really caring what he did with it.

Kirk Coleman

When I got home I called Chyna and cried as I broke the news to her. She never experienced such emotion from me, but today I didn't care. She came by with her family who stayed a while, then left her with me. As I lay there, I began to retrace my younger brother's life and the reason he died. At that time, place, and point, anything else meant nothing.

As the car rolled to a stop, a chorus of crickets awakened me, whistling in their highest pitch. The thick dew smelled of the South. The rich soil and the fragrant flowers toggled my memory to a time when I was young and ran freely. A lightning bug flew by blinking, lighting up only fragments of the still, dark night.

When I got myself together, I looked up and found were at Lola's house about 1 a.m. by my watch, but I knew it was midnight central standard time. Although this will always be Lola's house, Lola was not there. She died in the early '90s after a bout with cancer. She was a storehouse of mother's wit, who also raised her sister Inez's children, as well as many of her grandchildren. When she died, the duty of mentor, counselor, and guide was passed on to my mother, even though she lived far away in Detroit.

We knocked on the door at Lola's house, which was now occupied by her daughter Linda and her husband Robert. Robert answered the door. He was surprised, but glad to see us. I could tell he had had a little to drink, although I liked him better when he did. He was full of energy for that time of night.

Once when I was there, I went to the store and asked anyone if they wanted anything to drink and everyone there looked at me like I was crazy. I found out later that Linda didn't let him drink because it gave him too much courage; but to me, liquor gave his personality a boost. Since Linda was more than capable of kicking his ass (he weighed one hundred pounds soaking wet), Robert pretty much kept himself in check. He welcomed us and called Linda. We sat and talked for a while, then found our resting places for the night. I pulled my suit out to let it air from the long ride. I wanted it sharp-looking the next day. There I lay, trying to put together the pieces of a puzzle when I did not even know if all the pieces were there.

Chapter 5

When my parents moved back to Detroit in the early '60s, they stayed in the projects for a year, but I couldn't remember it. I was too young. What I did remember was the university, where I was raised until I was eight. My grandfather (my father's father) was a janitor at Wayne State University for thirty years. His loyalty and hard work enabled my parents the opportunity to live in and manage a large building with international students of all cultures. It was he whose name, Allen, I have as my middle name, and I am proud of it. It was he who spent, by location and circumstance, probably more time with us than any grandparent. It was he who passed along the distinguished brow and deep-set bedroom eyes that set DeMal and me apart from many. One of my earliest experiences with the church came from my grandfather, which could be his greatest achievement.

Jim and I were about five and three years old respectively when we first went to church with Granddad. We heard organ music, loud and rolling, for the first time. We sang hymns and watched others sing in praise for the first time. We saw others receive and experience the Holy Ghost for the first time—but wait! This was a bit too much for a three year old to fathom. Perhaps Granddad should have put us in the children's church, if one existed.

When we saw a man overtaken by a strange force that we had no prior knowledge of, it simply looked like he experienced the need to dance uncontrollably. Jim and I stared in amazement. Since Granddad was in the choir, we were alone in this experience, trying to understand. The man moved, shook, and gyrated in ways we, as children, had never seen before. Suddenly, to our astonishment, three large men subdued him as they struggled and wrestled him to the floor, then carried him out. For a young child unaccustomed to such an experience, I was in total shock. When we got home, I told Mother that we saw a fight at church. She laughed when she found out the truth.

* * *

When my parents were young, Granddad was the anchor of the Coleman family. He was old, wise, and kept his wife Jessie Coleman, my grandmother, in line. He was the sensible instrument used to keep my parents together, while being humorous with almost a cutting edge. He once told my father that whatever my mother "brings in the front door," he "takes out the backdoor."

Had it not been for my grandfather with his keen insight and wisdom, I doubt that my parents would have stayed together for so long. I only say that because when he died, my parents separated, divorcing shortly thereafter. Granddad knew my mother was a good woman and accepted her as his own daughter. He tried to keep things in order and sometimes would intervene trying to keep our family together when Dad went astray. He would meet us on campus halfway between Mackenzie Hall (where he worked) and our apartment. We would get in his '63 Biscayne (I'd love to have that car today) and stay over his and Grandma's house when my parents had to work.

Besides their house, the university campus was our playground. Jim and I would ride our bikes on the campus, throw Frisbees, and befriend college students. My love for animals began there too. We had a beagle named Lucky, gerbils, and a hamster, although not at the same time, of course.

Every time Dad would shower, shave, and get ready to leave, we would ask where he was going, and he would say, "I'm going to see a man about a dog," playing on our love for animals. (It turned out he was going to see a woman about a cat.) It did not take long to realize that Dad was not bringing a dog home. Dad knew that I loved animals. One day he found out just how much when he tried to get rid of our spotted beagle, Lucky. I was four at the time when he complained about disposing of Lucky, to our dismay. When he said, "Either I go or the dog goes," he fumed at my response.

"Dad, you go, but leave Lucky," was not what he expected to hear ...

"What the hell, boy! You rather have a dog than yo' daddy?"

"He's only a child, James," my mother responded, although she found it a bit humorous. "You see, you need to spend more time with the children," she added.

It was no surprise Lucky was gone soon after....

* * *

Detroit, Michigan. 1964-1968. Wayne State University. Macgregor Hall.

Although we lived inside the campus of the university, we went to public school outside in the projects district. Unlike today, the university had no school, so we mixed with the projects kids during school, and college students when we got out. What a life! University activities kept us going. The puppet shows, Charlie Chaplin silent movies, Punch and Judy, Hansel and Gretel, and parades going through the university district made for an interesting childhood. During the riots in Detroit in the '60s, we looked out the windows in amazement as tanks rolled by, rumbling the landscape and rattling the furniture.

The most interesting thing about the environment we lived in was that women from all over the world occupied a particular building. People called it an international female dorm. Dad, God bless him, must have felt like a bee in the dumpster of a syrup factory. At the same time, I discovered my attraction towards and appreciation of beautiful exotic women of all cultures. Some of these women escorted us to places in and around the university when Mom started working in 1966. They watched us while my parents were away; each one shared a dimension of her culture with us. Besides minor skirmishes, my parents got along okay, and we were still a happy family.

There were earth-shaking events in the '60s that toggled my memory in this place, incidents that changed the world in monumental proportions and, often times, took me away from childlike perspectives to a crash course in corruption, sadness, murder, and death, changing my world as well. The '60s were when I first learned to ride a bike and also learned that America, a country I called home, assassinated its leaders, like John F. Kennedy, Malcolm X, and Dr. Martin Luther King Jr. I was too young to read a newspaper, but I could see it all in my mother's eyes.

I remember when I was about two and saw Mom watching President John F. Kennedy's funeral. I saw her cry for the first time. We lived to see his son, John F. Kennedy Jr., die tragically in 1999, the final year of the century. It was here, also, that my family grieved for Martin Luther King and wondered what type of world this was becoming. As children do, we asked questions.

"Why would someone kill Martin Luther King, Mom? Did they hate him?" Jim asked, snuggling up next to Mom in front of the television.

"He never hurt anybody, did he, Mom?" I added.

"No, son. He didn't hurt anyone," she said, fighting tears. "I don't have the ...."

"Why, Mom?" I asked, looking for answers.

"Momma doesn't have all the answers, but I can tell you that all people are not good. Regardless of color, all people are not good."

When I broke my arm and Dad came by to see me in traction, I saw him cry for the first time. He was away when this happened. He probably thought that if he was home, it might have been avoided. I knew he loved us, but I could tell he was distracted by something. It was ironic that I did not understand at the time, because everybody said I was like him in many ways. Another irony is when I was born, Jessie, my half-white grandmother, God bless her, hinted to my father that, "Kirk is too dark. He might not be your son."

When my father approached my mother about this she responded, "James, read my lips. If you don't think Kirk is your son, sorry. I'll never try to convince you otherwise."

This is a woman who never cheated, remarried, or had a man after her divorce. The last and final irony of this whole matter was that, as I knew it, most meddling mothers-in-law came with a daughter. This rare case, however, came with a son.

Chapter 6

It was morning in Birmingham, and I heard movement in the house as I lay there for a moment, still stiff from the long ride. I could smell the aroma of a Southern breakfast and was soon out of bed, headed for the shower. I would wear my suit this day for the trip because it was not that far.

When I got to the dining room, what I saw looked like a plantation owner's feast. My cousin Linda had prepared three types of sausages—links, pan, and hot. She had grits with melted cheese. There were bacon, eggs, and biscuits, although I doubt the biscuits were homemade. That was okay though. Even though I could only compare this with highway food, it was magnificent. Mom used to cook breakfasts like this, with homemade biscuits or even "ho cakes" when we were all together, but now there was no need. I ate so much, I loosened my belt and tie, sat down, and dozed off.

When I woke up everyone was gone. I had the whole house to myself. Even so, I went outside to experience the southern spring morning. Sitting where Aunt Lola used to sit, I looked up the street where it sloped upward and disappeared in the distance, much like a dream.

Dreams were like this, I thought. *At least my own. Building up momentum and fading to reality as they peak, this sight looked familiar. How would it feel to live a dream out completely, or have I and just did not know and appreciate it?*

I wondered if following the blueprints of dreams would ever lead to my demise, casting aside the normalcy of life for things out of reach, out of touch, and beyond my own vanishing point. It was okay, I guess, to have aspirations as long as they didn't blind me to my surroundings, where I didn't recognize and appreciate what I already had. I thought DeMal would always be here, so I waited. Although I loved him, I just don't feel I loved him enough. When he was young, I was too busy trying to grow up myself. I was busy chasing skirts, and, if it was any consolation to me, so was he. *He would grow up some day and we would get along*, I thought. He was gone just ... like ...

that. There were so many things we put aside to live our lives, that we tended to forget the meaning of life itself. I was guilty of that in the first degree. Only now did I wish that the time I spent on the development and enrichment of a relationship had been spent on him.

Just like the weekend in 1989 when I was racing between my corporate job in Detroit and my new love, Chyna, in Tuskegee (who was originally from Detroit). She was the homecoming queen of her sorority. For a weekend that included one night in Tuskegee, one night in a posh Atlanta hotel, back to Tuskegee, then on to Detroit, I took my sporty rental car at speeds over 100 mph. During my trip, I noticed the Green Springs exit, which was less than five minutes away from Sook's house. This is what everybody called Aunt Lola. Stricken with cancer, she was at home, spending her last days with her family. In my haste, I procrastinated seeing my aunt alive the last time. Now sitting here on her porch, reflecting back to the past, I could not help but think about that.

When I got back to Detroit, two hours late, I went straight to work because I hadn't asked for Monday off—just Friday. Calvin, one of my bosses, was standing outside of the office complex as I drove up with a three-day beard shadow.

"Mr. Coleman, looks like you've had some weekend," he said.

"Yeah, ah, sorry, sir. I'm late, but I got stuck in traffic in Toledo. This is the first place I came."

Surprised, he said, "You mean you haven't been home yet?"

"No, sir," I responded.

He went inside, got my sales order book, then said, "Go home, shave, and get yourself together, Mr. Coleman."

I respected Calvin because for someone who accepted few mistakes and was always on me to be better, this time he understood and showed some compassion. Maybe it was because we were alone, away from brick and mortar of the complex that masked our true identity.

Calvin played the game better than most. He could infiltrate the ranks. Deep down inside of me, I knew he was the reason I was there. He hired me just months after I had returned from Atlanta in 1989. That was why I could never let him down. He took a chance on me. He rode my ass too. An ex-football, U of M, professional star turned corporate executive, he's black. It was obvious that he had to work harder than most to get to this point, so it was only fair to expect me to do the same. Wouldn't it be nice if the door always swung open this easy? It doesn't, and that's the way it is.

A mover and shaker, Calvin opened doors from employment to minority contracts, even during his own struggles for control and autonomy. That's why I always called him Mr. O' Neal—out of respect.

I took my sales book and drove home to clean up. This time I covered my ass. I kept my job and kept my woman miles away. In six months she would be done, home from college. I went back to my daily grind, thinking of the risks I took for the female species. To this day, I have yet to determine if this was a blessing or a curse.

It was 11:30 a.m. and already getting warm as the sun crept over the clouds in the "Heart of Dixie." This is what they called Alabama, although I disliked most Southern historical connotations. I decided to hang my suit jacket up on a hanger and put it on only when we got to our destination. Jim hadn't got back yet, but I remembered him telling me that he had to wash his car. I assumed he took Linda with him, because she was gone as well. Robert went to work. I was getting restless because I knew the trip was going to take two hours and we had to be there by 2:30 p.m. For many years, Birmingham had been our destination, but this time it was not. We were going deeper this time.

Compared to when my parents lived here, this place had changed dramatically over the years; now, only in a perfect world, was it the symbol of urban and social renewal.

I still see the flag, though.

You can buy a house, get married to your own kind, live a comfortable life, and want for little here.

I still see the flag.

You can open and run your own business and be very, very successful.

I still see the flag, bright red and robust. Even when I close my eyes, I see it.

The confederate flag is a symbol of the old South that failed to fade in the rebirth of the new South.

Today its only purpose seemed to be a tool of agitation, polarizing the people, either for or against it, for whatever reason. I truly believed there were some, although not many, who kept the flag in the closets of their mind, like a deceased grandfather's suit, with little or no ill intended. However, your grandfather's contributions, like my own, do not usually exceed the lines of your family. If his suit were in my closet, I would dispose of it. If, in this case, your grandfather's contributions adversely affected my family, I would burn his suit with contempt. This is your grandfather and not my own.

Although it was unintentional, I was in Atlanta when I first associated the flag with hate and fear. Atlanta was bustling in 1988, the year of the Democratic National Convention. People spilled out onto Marietta Street with their political agendas and signs of all shapes and sizes. The abortion people were there. The pro-people were there. The consumer advocate people were there. The Christian-flyer-handout people were there. The hate people were there.

After working for hours supervising the busy food service for the convention and dealing with thousands inside, I was rushing for the train home when I walked into this sea of agendas. I heard all of these arguments before and, today, did not feel like being bothered. However, I took a Christian flyer that asked, "Are you Saved?" and stuck it in my pocket as I headed to the Omni station. Walking toward my destination, I saw an increased police presence and what looked to be a riot starting. Moving nearer, I discovered it was the Ku Klux Klan.

My heart raced because I had never seen this group before except on television. I did not know exactly why I was drawn to the commotion. Perhaps it was curious sensationalism, the same reason kids were drawn to playground fights. Trying not to give them obvious attention, I approached the mob scene surreptitiously. *Why were they here?* I wondered. I knew I did not want to become obvious to them and play on their terms. I'd much rather play on my own. I cut and sliced my way through the angry crowd in my tuxedo until I stood almost face to face with pure racism. It was like being in the belly of hatred.

I could not respond quickly to what was happening in front of me. I just watched, in slow motion, each member that made up the group of four. I was not interested in the group as a whole because it was only as strong as its members. I zeroed in on one and chose to pick him apart to the lowest common denominator through analysis. I watched the green-eyed young man about thirty years old with the large sign that read, "Thank God for AIDS." How could he use God to promote a message so vile? Why would he think God would take his side against the innocent and afflicted? How could he hate people that he did not even know?

Unlike most of the crowd, I did not respond with hate. I just watched in awe, almost detached from the whole event. I may as well have been above it, looking down with a bird's- or God's-eye view. The rust-primer pickup was just what I expected. The rear window was emblazoned with the confederate flag, a gun rack inside, and white pride stickers on the bumper. In the South, I have seen many of them.

I continued my analysis of the young racist, trying to make sense of him. If the Bible says that I am to love my enemies, I can honestly say on this day, I fell short. Like an Aquarian dreamer, my mind drifted to the cause and present state of this situation.

The power of understatement took control of my imagination. No one had to tell me that he and I would never attend the same graduation, wedding, or funeral. No one had to tell me that, with the exception of a great catastrophe, his problems were his, and my problems were my own. Never shall the two meet. No one had to tell me that we would never live on the same street, have the same zip code, live in the same city, or attend the same church. With the incredible power of understatement, he told me what some might feel without thinking.

Although his views seemed rehearsed, like a grade school play, he was honest and did not hide behind a mask like some. If nothing else, I admired him for his honesty. For some reason, this "poor white trash" was starting to look like a Hemingway hero to me. Although I was almost there, I had to go further.

To love anything or anyone, you must first understand it. Once understood, the fear will dissipate and bring endless possibilities. Most people who dined with me never imagined that snails, sweetbreads, or squid could taste so good, if only given a chance. This was what I tried to do during this midday exposé on hate, although my need to understand surpassed my willingness to love.

Let's see, everybody loved kids and this green-eyed, scraggly, camouflaged gentleman was once one himself. *Where did this psychic wound begin?* I thought.

Certainly as kids, we had been alike in many ways. Like me, he probably had fears of the night and left his room to sleep with his mother. Like me, he pledged allegiance to a flag he knew little about. Like me, he wanted to know how he fit in the order of creation. He had hopes, dreams, fears, aspirations, and questions, just like me. He also probably wanted to know why people die and where they go. We were undoubtedly alike in so many ways; the answers to these questions were issued like marching orders, setting us on two different paths.

Going further back when he was developing in the womb of life, what were the conversations at the dinner table like? Were they an inwardly loving and outwardly hating environment or just simply dysfunctional? Did the parents know the people they hated? Did they have a reason for their actions? Was the hate based on negative experiences? Was fear involved? Did they say grace before they ate?

"*Trailer Trash!*" the crowd shouted.

"*Send me back to Africa, you cracker!*" someone added.

I was done. The crowd was getting violent and even the demonstrators realized that it was time to leave. They had more sense than I actually gave them credit for. I left myself, somewhat relieved that, although these people hated me and were honest about it, they were not in a position to affect me or limit my potential. They probably would never be in a position to affect me because they were too frank, too up front, and too darn honest. Today I was safe. I knew that the mask could be more complex than this, like an obstacle course clouded as opportunity.

Chapter 7

When I arrived in Atlanta the fall of 1981, I was fresh with hopes and dreams that had no limits. I scored advanced placement in English in an aptitude test and was advised to pursue it. Having studied fine and commercial arts in high school, I once had a vision of selling my art on a street corner. I did not particularly like this vision, so I decided not to study art in college. I would study English, get a degree, go to law school, Columbia or Northwestern, and practice Communications Law. These were my plans.

Although my parents were supportive, they were divorced by the time of my senior year of high school. It was actually a relief when they separated because times prior to that were often trying and turbulent. I worked for a year after high school to save money and planned to go to a black Baptist private school. Since I spent a great part of my life growing up on the largest university campus in Detroit, I needed to get away. Morehouse and Howard universities were my choices; I was accepted to both. Since I knew more people in the South than in Washington, D.C., I chose Morehouse. I knew I had to change from the Detroit job market to the Atlanta job market, which was rich, diverse, and challenging because I knew I had to work. Even though most of the people I went to school with did not work, I did not have the time or luxury to be like them. Honestly, I always thought I was middle class until I went to college during Reaganomics. I soon found out the truth.

By working nights as a desk clerk at my neighbor's motel in Detroit, my rent was paid six months in advance for a townhouse in the suburbs of Atlanta. I opted to stay off campus to save money because the cost of room and board was extremely high. In doing so, I had more freedom, more responsibility, more control of my life, and more time to come up with money. Marzell, my roommate, was a year older. We shared our first of two six-month leases. For the most part, my transition from Detroit to Atlanta went fine. We just found that we forgot to plan for one important necessity when we got to Atlanta—eating.

During the start of the second week in 1981 when tuition was paid and money was getting low, we bought a bag of potatoes and cooked them in many different ways: Monday, we had French fries; Tuesday, potatoes au gratin; Wednesday, hash browns; Thursday, homemade potato chips; Friday, we ran out of ideas and had fries again; Saturday, we had money wired from home. By Monday, it was time to find a "JAY- O- BEE"—a job.

After class Monday, Marzell and I went our separate ways to find employment. He found a job.

"I got hired at the Atlanta Airport Marriott," he said.

"What do you do?" I asked.

"Busboy, which means I get tips," he said excitedly.

I nodded my head in agreement. "Cool, what is the restaurant called?"

"I think it is called 'La Café.' It has a Mexican theme."

"Is that the only restaurant around?" I did not want to live with, go to school with, and also work with Marz. (He was big and sometimes pushy when he didn't get his way, so I wanted to give him his space.)

"Nah, there's a real fancy restaurant where the waiters wear tuxedos right next to it. They even use the same kitchen area, but it's down on the other side," he said.

After being "potatoed out" for the last week, Marzell and I were thrilled to find out that hotel employees made tips and ate free with full benefits. Marz told me that the hotel and restaurant were hiring and suggested I go the next day after class.

Never before has anyone been so excited about getting a busboy position, but we were nineteen and twenty years old, and although this was not our first job, it was our first job in Atlanta. I wanted desperately to be free from calling home collect and asking Mom for money. She had divorced Dad two years prior and had the weight of the world on her shoulders. Her hip was starting to bother her; surgery was imminent. She still worked because she had to. I almost resented my father because I thought he should have tended the home front while I was away. The outside forces finally took a toll on him, and he was gone. Fortunately, Jim was still home for now, and DeMal was growing up faster than a weed. When he was thirteen years old, he wore a size fourteen shoe.

Hunger, anticipation, and my studies kept me up most of the night, so I prayed (on my knees) that I would get the job I desperately needed. After class I went to the hotel, which was a short distance from the airport. Unlike Marzell, I was hired in the three-star, gourmet restaurant called "Bentley's." It was a beautifully elegant restaurant, where the waiters prepared some items tableside on a heated garradon. The beauty of my job was that I did not bus tables, but still made tips—very good ones. My job title was "Aisle Attendant." When the waiters had special orders like oysters, Rumboozil, Bananas Foster, Cherries Jubilee, or French onion soup, I would prep and sometimes serve them. I was dressed like a waiter in black and white, with an apron that fell almost to my ankles. I also worked the aisle with the cooks, assisting in both the front and back of the house. For my first gig in Atlanta, I, like old folks used to say, "hit the nail on the head."

The only thing I did not particularly care for was that I had to shuck oysters when the chef made Oysters Rockefeller, or when the waiters served them fresh. Oysters were said to be beneficial to the sex drive, which is why many men seemed to make them a staple for an appetizer. One night a businessman ate two dozen raw! After sticking myself a few times, I finally got the hang of shucking. I kept shucking and shucking, thinking that, one day, I might find a pearl, although I knew it was unlikely.

The oyster is an amazing delicacy from an amazing Creator. It is a profusion of sand and sea that holds its cargo so tightly that it has to be pried open with a sharp tool. Inside the crusty, rigid, and dangerously sharp protective surface lies a membrane so delicate, it even slides down your throat. Floating on a bed of its own self-preserving liquid, the oyster is anchored by a ligament that keeps it securely in place, like a mother's womb.

In the kitchen, I would watch the chef, Leonard, prepare delicacies and French sauces that were new to my senses and palate. Yes! I could eat, and eat well, I might add. My culinary skills were also improving as I replicated the restaurant dishes at home to my friends' amazement. I also found other ways to prepare potatoes, of course.

Bentley's staff was a close-knit group made up of all types: from chiropractic students, foreign exchange students, to seasoned, professional waiters. Most of the waiters were gay, but too handsome and in demand to be pushy and flirtatious towards others. Thank God! I was grateful that I was chosen to complement this diverse mix. *(Thinking back, I did wear a pinkish Polo tie to the interview. Ah hah!)* This environment was cosmopolitan and relaxed, where everyone treated each other with respect. This diversity created a system of checks and balances that made the workplace harmonious. For instance, if you made a demeaning statement about Arabs, Hussein and Amir would be offended. If you made a demeaning remark about Jews, Paul, the chiropractor student, would be offended. For whites, John or the manager, Mr. Carder, may be offended. For blacks, Larry, Ernie, Kenric, Howard, and I could be offended. For women, Marilyn, the lone female waiter, would be offended. (There were not many women in gourmet restaurants at this time. I don't know why, but I do know that the trays could get quite heavy.) No bigots were allowed. If you made offensive remarks toward anyone gay, be prepared for anyone out of these groups to confront you. Better yet, be prepared to leave.

    This is a perfect environment to represent all types of people, ideas, views, and beliefs. That is why the United Nations is so effective, because of the mix. I would hate to work or live in an environment where I was a minority in a sea of whites. Every whisper would draw my attention. I don't care if it is black, white, or Latino—I do not like monopolies.

The larger corporations could benefit from this utopian environment and often receive incentives to encourage the proper mix. Private industry, such as family-run operations, reserves the right to hide under the complexities of choice, criteria, and qualifications, if they so desire. Unlike Ford Motor Company, they are not directly under the microscope. The truth is there are still some limited diversity businesses, with the exception of the lone warehouse worker who may be a minority. In metro Detroit, one of the nation's most polarized areas and its bustling suburbs, to my amazement, I have seen many such businesses.

Giving a full two-sided view to the subject, some individuals are not in the corporate American workplace by their own choice. Some are powerbrokers in their own right who harbor feelings that are militant to today's standards of acceptance. Many of today's young entrepreneurs are brilliant individuals who excel in their own domain. They could complement the corporate culture, but choose to resist it for their own reasons. In a conversation with Dylan Womack, my friend from high school and college, I found that education could also create isolation from the much-accepted corporate culture.

Dylan is an example of brilliance and creativity within the guise of his own chosen domain. Having studied English with him at Morehouse, he had provided me with years of challenging and often militant thought from the abstractions of Emily Dickinson to the anger of Claude McKay. I found this conjecture to be beneficial, therapeutic, and enlightening. Everyone needs someone like Dylan when they become too complacent, too passive, and too at ease with the norm. Many people wanted the respect and attention that this brilliant mind tried to avoid, but few could share the same stage with him. The son of a doctor/lawyer, who graduated from law school himself, he did not practice for his own reasons.

"Kirkwood, any time you have someone who rapes or kills and can get out of jail in ten or fifteen years and walk the streets, while someone who supports his family selling drugs and gets put in jail for life, then something is wrong," said Dylan. "In my law, if you rape someone, you die. In my law, if you kill someone, you die! I am an attorney, but I choose not to take part in this system. I just want to be left alone to handle my business and raise my sons," he said.

Although Dylan's views were more radical than my own, it seemed that somehow we were always in accord, as if my own harbored thoughts were put into his words. He was the mouthpiece for what was kept deep inside the corridors of my mind, shared with few, so I gravitated towards him. To some, Dylan appeared angry. Unlike Dylan, my anger was exposed only in a fit of rage, but was there, nonetheless, close to the surface.

Perfectly content owning The Billiard Gallery, a poolroom full of African art with a bar, Dylan and his brother, Bonnie, imported and distributed major pieces of art from Africa, while displaying and selling them in their place of business. Not surprisingly, it was one of the most unique concepts for a bar I have ever seen; Dylan was ahead of his time. Detroit's blue-collar history and burgeoning technological growth were not quite ready for a concept so unique, but the Womack brothers stood true to their concept with a select clientele. I use the word *select* only because if Dylan did not like you, he would throw you out.

Like other establishments in the Harmonie Park area, my company, Encore Group, was the in-house choice for catering at the Billiard Gallery. When I called Dylan to congratulate him when the new ballpark's construction was moved next to his location, he was not thrilled with the idea of mixing with whites, even though his business would surely increase. He has moved since then. His business included major contracts, real estate, imports, and setting up a timeshare for property in Africa.

"Kirkwood," he always called me, "I sell and display authentic African masks. You also know how I feel about white people. My great-grandmother died when I was sixteen years old, and I talked with her a lot. Kirkwood, her mother was a slave, and she told me the whole story, the fear, the rapes, the whole nine yards. I don't hate them. I just want to be left alone."

"I feel you," I replied.

There were, indeed, times I wanted to be left alone like an island with no peninsulas or bridges.

There were times when I did think I could change the world with a dose of my own elixir, only later, retreat into a silo of isolated indifference.

If you saw Dylan, you might mistake him for who he is not. The proudly worn Afro or braids and beads could give the impression of one making a last-ditch pitch for his heritage.

He doesn't wear a mask though.

The expensive German sedan, minus the suit and tie and the focused anger, may lead you to confuse him with Detroit's drug underworld.

Please don't make that mistake.

Displaying a sincere openness to some, while being abrasive to others may lead some to think he is armed and dangerous.

He is.

People make the same mistake everyday at Detroit stoplights when they size people up that they do not even know. In Dylan's case, some may never know better.

He doesn't wear a mask. He just imports them.

* * *

I was getting bored and somewhat angry that Jim was not back yet. It was approaching noon, but I knew that Jim was on his own schedule. That was okay with me because I recognized that the people who counted on him most, that is, his family, could depend on him. I could always depend on him being a little late, even though he liked to rush me. It didn't take me long to gauge that when he said fifteen minutes, he meant an hour. Now we had complete understanding.

In the distance I could see the green Acura finally coming over the hill, gleaming in the light of day. As I thought, Jim and Linda went to get the car cleaned. It must have been full service since it took so long. We wasted no time leaving. Even though we had a map on hand, neither of us knew where we were going. The map didn't help much. Minters, our destination, wasn't even on the map. We only knew it was somewhere outside Selma. We needed extra time in case we got lost. We were sure to.

We left our other clothes in Birmingham where we would come back that night for a party in our honor. Although we lived in Detroit, this is where all, or most, of our family lived and was from. Uncle Seright, (pronounced "See-right"), the oldest of my mother's siblings, had to leave the area first in the late '50s for Chicago. Being in the Air Force, he'd traveled to many places, including France, Spain, Germany, and Italy. He found it hard to adjust to coming home to Birmingham, Alabama, in the late '40s. He could not readjust to the limitations of the South and was making enemies too quickly for a man his age.

He once told an insurance man who was white to take off his hat when he came into Granddad's house. My uncle knew the consequences of leaving your hat on in a white man's house. He only asked the man to show some respect. After all, he was coming to collect money. The insurance man turned red with anger, took off his hat, collected the money, and left. Everyone knew it was time for Uncle Seright to leave.

One day he caught a bus to Chicago and never looked back.

Out of four girls, my mother was the only one to leave the South. She is also the only survivor of the daughters. If this meant anything, I'm glad she left. Today when she visits the South, she is treated like royalty by her nieces and nephews and their children, who adopted her as a mother figure. When we come, we are welcomed warmly as well.

* * *

We got on Highway 65 going to a place where we had only been once when we were kids. In 1972 my parents rented a large motor home and took us on a two-week vacation. Jim was eleven, I was nine, and DeMal was two. We went from Birmingham to Orlando, including stopovers at Minters, Alabama, and Sanford, as well as Pensacola, Florida, visiting every relative in between. In Minters I remember the family log cabin house. I had never seen one before or since. In Pensacola I saw a gust of wind, presumably a tornado, take the roof off a house in seconds.

Our destination this time, however, was not sunny Florida. It was deep, backwoods Alabama, the home of red soil, sugarcane, and Southern hospitality. The sun was sweltering; I became very uncomfortable when we left the artificially cool climate of Jim's car. In this simple environment, I felt out of place in a button-up shirt, tie, and lizard shoes, but we now had to mix and mingle with locals to find how to get to our destination. This was the country, indeed, where a shopping mall consisted of a supermarket, a drugstore, a McDonald's, and some extra parking. For the extreme heat, the choice of attire seemed to be a plaid short sleeve shirt or a tank top, accompanied by jeans and boots. The people seemed nice though. Somehow I immediately felt that the people knew we were foreigners from a faraway place. Since Jim was driving, I let him worry about talking to people. My task was to find something wet and cool to quench our thirst. It seemed like a sweltering 90 degrees already.

"Are you thirsty," I asked Jim.

"Yeah."

"You get directions, and I'll get something to drink."

Although the store had Mountain Dew, I was looking for something frozen this time. In Detroit, some stores had frozen Mountain Dew in the summer, but we were not in Detroit. I took two large cups from the dispenser at the slush machine and filled them with cherry slush all the way to the top, being careful not to make a mess. In Kentucky, on the way here, a clerk came from behind the counter after I got cappuccinos for Jim and me. She came out wiping the counter frantically, as if I made a mess. The funny thing is I can't remember doing so. Who knows? Maybe something else was bothering her.

Chapter 8

We left, taking the rural route through Alabama to Selma. Jim drove confidently and seemed to now know where he was going. The younger-brother-reliance mechanism kicked in. I was free to gaze out the window and take in all the sights, as if my eyes were the cameras of a documentary. *I was not just younger; I was the baby again*, I thought. It was just Jim and me once more. Although I hated being introduced as the baby when I was a child, the thought that I was the youngest now was staggering. Sometimes I think too much.

I gazed out the window as we journeyed through the rural passages of the South. Only fifty miles from

Birmingham and fifty miles to go, yet so different in comparison to the large southern city we just left.

This is so different than Detroit, I thought, since I had to adjust my vision from a congested vertical to a wide-open horizontal view to take in the sights. Mankind's creations of brick and mortar were upstaged by God's works of agricultural magnificence, consisting of newly blossoming greenery, budding plants, and expecting trees bearing fruit. Growing up here appeared to be a carefree experience, without the stress and violence I became used to growing up back home. I wondered how my life would have been different growing up in the South. Would I need guns, attack dogs, or even a reputation here?

Like my Doberman pinscher, Sabre, my ears were always up, ready to intervene if Mom and Dad squared off in marital discord. Even as a child, I would not allow anyone to touch my mother in my presence. Once I got between my parents and knocked my Dad on the couch. At the same time, I had to maintain a reputation at school to insure a safe walk home. Dad always told me to beat up the toughest guy in the group. This psychology worked in grade school. It proved better than working my way up the hierarchy of toughness.

Growing up, I fought more with older boys than with those my age because the older ones wanted respect, and I didn't feel that age was reason enough to command respect. I kept Jim, my older brother, working in my defense, because I was the youngest of a generation of boys in a neighborhood of developing gangs and criminals that was relying more on guns. It was a nice place to live though, and despite any obstacles we encountered, this was middle, working-class life in Detroit, Michigan.

Detroit, Michigan. The summer of 1972.

One day Jim and I learned an important lesson on survival from Dad that shaped us for a lifetime. It was while Mom was at work at the post office, and he made one of his rare appearances as a father at home, watching DeMal, who was only two years old. He showered, shaved, and got dressed like he usually did when working at the university, but for some reason he was home today.

I went around the block to visit a friend, Dwayne, who was a year older than I, but closest to my age in the neighborhood. Suddenly, I heard a nearby door burst open, and Mark came out the house, screaming, and running in my direction.

"*AAAAAHHH! I'm gonna get you, Coleman boy!*"

Even though I could not recall what I did to deserve this, I turned and bolted for home. I was ten years old, and since Mark was almost four years older, he was closing in on me like a cheetah on a wounded antelope. His screams were getting closer and closer; even though I knew that I would not make it home, the closer I got to my house, the less severe the consequences would be. As I was running and he was closing in, I thought of why he was after me.

A few weeks prior to this incident when we were playing baseball, he recklessly brandished a gun and was getting cocky with it. Immediately he felt the power. He looked around the crowd of ten boys for their reaction to his newfound power and reacted to their fear. When he told someone to *"Shut up!,"* I knew it was time to leave. I slipped away and told my mother. She told another neighbor, Mrs. Brown, who called his grandmother with whom he lived. Even though I did what I thought was right, to him, I was a snitch, and he was out for revenge. With this in mind, I tried desperately to elude capture, because I didn't know if he carried the gun or not. I could hear his steps now behind me as I was nearing my block, but I was too far away from home to avoid capture. As I made it to the first house on my block, I cut across the grass, and at that moment, he pounced on me. When I turned over to defend myself, he put his knee in my chest and started punching and kicking me like a madman, screaming the whole time. He pummeled me for about fifteen seconds, which seemed much longer. After the last kick, I curled up and clutched my stomach, pretending to be hurt, so he finally left.

Although I was only seven houses away from home, it was a long walk back there. Upon arriving, I wanted to cry, but I knew Momma wasn't home. It was good she wasn't. When Dad asked me what happened, I burst into tears and told him that Mark jumped me and kicked me in the stomach. He shouted out some profanities, called Jim, and told us to get in the car with the baby in the front seat. We took off in the '67 Ford Esquire station wagon with dad driving like I'd never seen him drive before. We were looking for Mark, but neither of us knew what Dad had in mind. When he saw Mark walking home, he pulled alongside him and slammed on the brakes.

"Hey, boy! Why the fuck don't you fight someone your own damn age," Dad said.

"Uh–huh," Mark replied, not knowing what to say.

Yeah, get him, Dad, I thought.

I assumed it was over ... but it wasn't. Dad parked the car, turned to us, and gave the orders for our assignment.

"Either you kick his ass or I'm kicking yours until my nose bleeds," he said to us.

Jim and I looked at each other and knew what we had to do. It was something about how he said what he said that registered to me as "do or die." "Until my nose bleeds" meant that he would kick our asses for a *very* long time, since I've never known my Dad's nose to bleed. I already got my ass kicked once this day, and that was enough. We had to win this one.

We got out of the car despite our fears and circled Mark like two hyenas ready to make a kill. The predator was now the prey; it was he that swallowed the bitter pill of fear as he tried to elude capture, but was too proud to run. He swung at Jim, who being the strongest one, grabbed him in a bear hug. I moved in to inflict damage by punching him twice in the head. Jim started choking him, and, like a predator, I went for his legs, knocking them from under him. When he fell, he landed on the sidewalk with Jim on top, taking the air out of him. While he was down, I stepped on his head and kicked him repeatedly in the face with my blue canvas Converse All Stars until his nose bled. My fear was replaced with adrenaline.

"Okay, that's enough," Dad said, eyes almost smiling, reveling in victory himself.

I was almost starting to enjoy the assault, the power, the thirst for blood—the frenzy. I heard about it, knew it existed, and this was the closest I came to it. It was exhilarating. Why would he bring me back? This was what he wanted, wasn't it? It was more than getting even now. I wanted to get ahead. Why did Dad call off the pack?

"Alright! That's it," he said forcefully.

We stopped. Dad knew we proved our point, and he did not want us to hurt Mark seriously. My fear was gone, that day at least. I was too young to know it would rekindle itself as a primary component of survival throughout my life. Today, I learned a lesson about revenge, and it was sweet indeed. Tomorrow, I would learn diplomacy, but not today. We beat the neighborhood bully to a pulp while overcoming our fears, not because we were bullies, but because he deserved it, and my Dad gave us no other choice.

We got back into the station wagon like two gangsters that made their hit. DeMal, only a baby, looked on with excited eyes. Dad, I could see through the rearview mirror, was proud of us. He won through us. This situation would have been totally different if

Mom were home. Calls would have been made instead of fighting. That explains why every boy needs a father figure, even if it is short term.

Despite neighborhood rivalries in our immediate area, all of us were still friends. Some of these friendships still exist today because some of my friends still exist. On the other hand, I have witnessed a virtual extinction of young outlaws who took revenge, rivalry, and gunplay too far. Guys called Pookie, Huck, Doll Baby, Larry B., and Willie McCloud were known as "8 Mile" throughout the neighborhood. They were armed and dangerous and stayed across a large field known as the "army camp," which separated two different types of real estate and two different types of living.

Everyone knew that crossing the "army camp" could bring about immediate danger. After all, these guys made Mark, my nemesis, look like a church mouse. He avoided them as well. We took risks, however, since most of the good restaurants were on Eight Mile Road. Jim and I never got jumped, but some of my friends were robbed and roughed up. Mom worked with Huck's mom, which gave us some security in their territory, but not much.

One day in the late Michigan fall in the early- to mid-'70s, some of those fellows visited us from the other side of the field. It was a cold, brisk, sunny afternoon, with more leaves on the ground than on the trees. The days were getting shorter and shorter; by 5:30 p.m., it was dark. We were playing football with the neighborhood boys. There must have been fifteen or sixteen of us. Even the older boys were there, some five or six years older than me. Despite our rivalries, we played a good competitive game with no fights. As usual, I was the youngest one there. We played on our side of the "army camp," the side closest to where we lived.

Suddenly, in the distance, we saw about twelve guys approaching who asked to see the football. They took it and insisted on playing—them versus us. They were dangerous looking, swinging nunchakus (sticks on a cord or chain made popular from Bruce Lee movies), and miniature baseball bats. I knew it was likely that at least one of them was strapped. Ultimately, confirming my fears, one of them, the leader, took a silver object from the front of his pants and put it in a coat on the sideline. These boys seemed much older than us. A few of them could have been eighteen or nineteen years old. We consented to their terms because no one was in a position to refuse. We were hostages and too scared to say "no."

Where was Huck? I thought, trying to score points on diplomacy. We didn't know any of these guys, so I knew we were in big-time trouble.

When the game began, they were compulsively and excessively violent. They cheated, elbowed, and hit us after some plays were made. They were winning by a large margin, but the truth was they were not good football players at all. Most of them lacked the discipline and finesse to play the sport.

They were only intent on hurting us, and we were too scared to hurt them.

In our huddle, we discussed ways to avoid an outcome that was imminent—getting beaten after the game. I only wished Dad would come by and tell us to come home for whatever reason, but he wasn't home today.

"Let's play for a while; soon it will be dark, and they should be ready to quit," said Teddy in the huddle.

"Watch me. I'm going long," whispered Cecil.

The play started. Bubba, getting elbowed in the face, got angry, so the play was stopped. Cecil kept going long, longer, longer. He ran off the field and kept running towards home. He looked back grinning as he jubilantly ran for his life, free from harm. He also outsmarted us—his own teammates. He didn't even send help. *So much for unity*, I thought.

This situation was getting out of hand. As long as Jim and I could get out of there, my friends were on their own. When self-preservation kicked in, I was only worried about my brother's safety and that of my own, although I didn't want to see anyone get hurt. I once heard my grandfather, Allen Coleman, say, "I'd rather be a live coward than a dead hero." I knew exactly what he meant.

"What we gonna do, Jim?" I asked, thinking he might have a solution.

"I dunno. Either fight or run and take our chances."

"How 'bout we run first, and fight only if we have to," I mumbled.

"How 'bout it? Jim replied, almost under his breath.

We were just no match for these guys, I concluded, after seeing our biggest guy pummeled by two of their smallest. Some of them had facial hair—beards—while I, at twelve, spent hours looking in the mirror waiting for individual hairs to grow.

When we scored, we devised a plan. It was all we had left. During the kickoff, we would throw the ball downfield over their heads and run—home—in the opposite direction. They could even have the football. When Brian, our strongest one with the strongest arm, threw the ball, we bolted. Jim and I were out'a there. All our team took off, headed home. Our opponents, being the brutes they were, fell for this trick, but were soon in pursuit of us. The plan gave us enough distance on them that even the slowest of us should have gotten away. But Brian Johnson, known as "Pretty Boy," who either had further to run home or did not run fast enough, didn't escape. The gang took their wrath out on him. Being half-white with a curly, sandy brown Afro, he was a feast for the hungry wolves; he was the sacrificial lamb that took the asswhooping that we all missed. It was bad, I heard. He survived it though. They beat him with miniature baseball bats and nunchakus until he was unconscious. He was hospitalized three days for a concussion. We all knew it could have been any one of us.

Kirk Coleman

The blood-for-blood sport that these young men lived by grew increasingly violent when revenge was involved. As they conquered their own neighborhoods with fear, they soon ventured out to challenge others farther away in a reign of terror. Blood-for-blood ultimately resulted in a life-for-life policy. The neighborhood legends now existed only in conversations of the surviving few. Like Jessie James, some went out "guns a blazing," while others didn't know what hit them.

For me, this was the time I would learn diplomacy. I learned many things from these young men who are here no longer. The most important lesson was I did not want to be like them, live like them, or die like them. *Choosing to live by the pen would, in turn, give me more options,* I thought. There were erasers, white-out, or simple rewrites available. The sword was my last resort, my defense mechanism used only when the pen did not work or was ignored. When some people say, "I'm about to get ghetto-up in here," they feel they have exhausted all known means of expression. A ghetto is a limited environment with limited means. Channeled anger is much more effective than an outburst, I find. What if people kicked it up a notch and said, "I'm about to get boardroom-up in here, or legislative- or legal-up in here?" Where would they be? The jails and cemeteries are full of violent offenders who didn't consider their options. To me, wise is he who learns from his own mistakes, but wiser is he that learns from the mistakes of others. Sometimes the stakes are too high to make your own mistakes.

Chapter 9

I watched attentively as the rural industrial landscape gave way to rich, bountiful agricultural scenes. The road we traveled on was the only separation for the fields of peach trees that faded to the east and west in perfect, well-formed lines. In the distance, I saw an old tractor that stopped apparently years ago, collecting the remnants of age and time. Like a soldier that died on the battlefield, this was its final resting place. The weeds had finally won the battle with the old tractor, almost concealing it from view. The engine door swung open, revealing that missing parts had probably been transplanted to power another.

Like a dead soldier, it lay stripped without shoes or musket, unable to perform its duties.

I often think about my great-grandfather, "Crack" Oscar Smith, the Indian. The South was starting to look more like it did when he lived here. Although I am not sure what tribe he was from, one of my aunts told me he was of Seminole descent. I eagerly accepted this without skepticism because the Seminole tribe had a proud history of fierce resistance. This was all I had. My mother's grandfather, he had long, fine, dark hair braided down his back. A short, stocky, left-handed man clad in overalls and untied "brogans" (boots), he was eccentric even in his own time. The freckles that decorated his olive complexion were passed down his family lines to Mom's siblings. I love freckles. Uncle Seright, my mother's brother in Chicago, mirrored this mystical character more than anyone else did.

"Crack" left no photographs of pictures with dignitaries. There was no diary or guide to keep the good family name. There was no map to unearth some hidden fortune. He didn't have much, but whenever he saw his grandkids, he had either penny candy and, or a kind word. His history is oral. He respected the land in Fort Deposit and used it harmoniously—not for ill-gotten gain, industry, or enterprise. Like clockwork, he would leave home in the early spring before planting and would not return until late fall, after harvest, and he never talked much about his travels. In fact, he never even said goodbye. He just vanished and reappeared like a ghost. Some, like his son-in-law, T. K. Lampkin, my mother's father, even called him a hobo because he traveled more than he worked. Venturing throughout the South by foot and train, he is said to have traveled as far as Florida.

The Indian spirit, illustrated by my great-grandfather, was a proud, complex spirit that knew no geographical barriers. Too vast and too restless to be confined to a plantation, or even a home, it is obvious native Americans were not good for the early American colonial tapestry. As the French author and American critic, Freneau, wrote in his poem, "The Indian Burying Ground," the spirit knows no rest, even in death. This annual ritual was part of my great-grandfather's life until he died in 1955. He even left his deathbed in an attempt to leave town, but was stopped, this time, by his family. After his death, his wife, Molly Anne Porterfield Smith, was visited by his children from afar, who she never even knew existed. His daughter, my great-aunt Ida, took most of what is known about this man to her grave just before I cared to inquire. This, unfortunately, was all I knew about my great-grandfather.

What I remember about my Aunt Ida dates back to my childhood in the early '70s, while visiting Chicago for Mom's cousin Mitt's funeral. Mitt, my mother's first cousin or her father's sister's son, loved coming to Detroit with Uncle Seright. When he did come, he would go and fill-up our refrigerator with everything good. His favorite was fried perch with spaghetti and Mom's homemade meat sauce made with onion, green pepper, diced tomatoes, celery, and 100 percent ground beef. For dessert, we would have blackberry cobbler topped with French vanilla ice cream. Mitt loved to eat. He was also tickled to disbelief over the lanky, fair-skinned, reddish-brown curly-haired baby DeMal, who said and did the funniest things. In fact, he even willed DeMal one thousand dollars when he died.

Mitt's death brought me to the first funeral I would attend. I was too young to attend my mother's father's funeral in Birmingham, although we still took the trip. My other grandfather, Allen Coleman, had yet to pass, so I was new to funerals—not even twelve years old.

As if the funeral was not enough, other things happened as well. When we first pulled into the chapel, it had a sign for "drive-through viewing." Puzzled, I pulled on Jim's arm and asked for an explanation.

"Jim, what is drive-through viewing?" I asked.

"Well, you just pull up to the window and look at dead people, that's what you do," Jim answered, nodding his head and looking self-assured.

Jim had all the answers. He was probably trying to scare me even though he was probably scared himself over something so eerie—so ridiculous. This was his first funeral as well. Could it be that people were in such a rush that they must do a drive-by on the dead? Well, what about the late night, after-work viewer who comes, say, at 1:00 a.m.? Who thought of this idea anyway? It was morbid, apparently untested, bound for failure, and was scaring the hell out of me. To a curious kid or seasoned adult who wanted to sleep nights, this was a bit much.

Added to the drama of the funeral experience in Chicago, the funeral car, a Cadillac limousine, was stolen from the lot. Welcome to Chicago. Also, during the procession, one car slammed into the back of another on the freeway, causing major damage. For a man who lived such a peaceful existence, all hell seemed to break loose at Mitt's funeral.

During the service, I found myself seated next to Aunt Ida, who came all the way from Alabama to attend. When she hugged me, I noticed how big and firm her breasts were. They were like two missiles ready to launch and my small, twelve-year-old body seemed to fit in between them; I liked them. Mom said she was once a beautiful, fair-skinned, green-eyed knockout in her day with "plenty men." Married five times with just one son, Mizell, everyone in Birmingham seemed to know someone Ida was married to or was dating.

Being my mother's aunt, Ida was the closest thing to a mother figure for her. Ida was my Mom's mother's sister. She would watch them as kids while my Mom's father, T. K. Lampkin, worked at the steel mill. Aunt Ida would send them outside unattended while she entertained male guests for hours at a time. As a little girl, my mother prayed that she would *not* be like Aunt Ida, and I'm glad she prayed that way. In the close-knit Southern community in the early '40s, my aunt had the reputation for having "more men than Fido had gnats on his ass." Ida did introduce my Mom to church at a young age although Ida dated, married, and divorced the assistant pastor of the church within two years. My aunt typifies the temptations of a beautiful, yet unanchored woman in the South. For some strange reason, the darker the man, the more he loved, wooed, and tempted her.

Everything seemed to be going okay, or as well as could be expected for a funeral. As the organ music played its highs and lows, so went people's emotions. Aunt Ida was posturing. People were crying, but to themselves. Ida was positioning. Suddenly she started sobbing in her deep throaty voice.

"Lawd, why'd you haf to take him? Why, Lawd? Why?!"

I looked at her and then straight ahead, trying to prepare for what was to come.

"Oh, no!" she screamed in her deep throaty voice. She continued, "Lawd Jesus, Why? Why? Why? No, Jesus, oh, no! God, no! Jesus, why?"

I was on pins and needles at the time, sitting up straight with my legs closed tightly. In my mind, I wished Jesus would have told her something to make her calm down or, at least, answered her question, not for everyone to hear—just her. Hearing His voice would have been a bit too much for a twelve year old to take since Billy Graham already scared me enough.

Ida continued screaming and flailing her arms shouting, "Lawd, Jesus, God, No! Why? Why? Why?!!"

In her fit, she hit me in the chest, knocking the air out of me.

This was not a pleasant experience for my first funeral. I was stunned over so much activity; I was weak and exhausted and my chest hurt. After the ladies in white brought her fit under control, Ida sat there quietly and said nothing else the whole time. I found out, only later, she did this at everyone's funeral. This was her recreation. Since then, the only time I've seen Aunt Ida has been at a funeral, and I've always been careful to sit a few rows back since our first funeral encounter. She could have told me everything I wanted to know about my great-grandfather "Crack," but I never asked.

* * *

On my Dad's mantel lies a black-and-white photo of a man who is his grandfather. He is proud of his grandfather because he knew him personally and this was his grandfather by blood. This was his mother, Jessie Small's, father. Jessie Small married my grandfather, Allen Coleman, in Minters, Alabama, and moved to Birmingham and then Detroit in the late '50s. I never asked why the man's picture was displayed so proudly in the center of the mantel. I paid it no mind. My emotions are quite different from when I first saw it, and I have reason. My great-grandfather is unquestionably white. A tall, lanky, somewhat distinguished-looking man with round wire-rimmed glasses, he looked as if he could be both kind and compassionate or bring an element of fear to his adversaries. I found he could do both. I was foolish to think that this historical, mystical figure was locked away in time in the world of black-and-white snapshot photos, never to effect me. What did a white farmer and storeowner in the early 1900s have to do with me? My world was panoramic, living color, and three-dimensional. His was not.

He is my great-grandfather though, and I cannot change anything about that. It is society more than myself that tells me we have little in common. My grandmother's father is a stranger. My father's grandfather is a stranger. My great-grandfather is a stranger. When do they end and when do I begin in this gene pool of Russian roulette? Somehow the words *privilege, deception,* and *advantage* keep coming to mind. We must make the statistician's job easier at whose convenience?

Folks in the South used to say that it was not good for blacks and whites to mix and reproduce because, even without considering the elements of rejection, acceptance, and confusion, our genes just didn't mix positively.

"Black and white blood should not be mixed. When they do, the children inherit the worst of each race," some said.

Even though blood is red, perhaps fear was the catalyst for this belief. Today, it is ignorance and hysteria. Although there are some black and white people who may agree with this today, there is no proof to support this belief in any glossy medical journal that I know.

Why do mixed people appear to have some of the most unique and attractive features, like rich colorful skin and beautiful hair? My friend Dwayne has some of the most beautiful, well-mannered, disciplined kids I have ever seen. Married for fifteen years and in love with his wife, this made all the difference. I can only speculate what he went through to get to this point, but he is wiser as a result of it.

Lena Horne and Halle Berry are beautiful by universal standards of acceptance, yet they are mixed. Sadly, but seriously, you can always, then and now, obtain a beautiful "mixed" child at an adoption agency near you. Mixing, or mating without love is pure deception. Without love, planting a seed is nebulous, like a tulip shoot in a cold, dark, arctic climate.

We were entering the city of Selma, which made most of the landscape we crossed pale by comparison. A large city, it seemed cut out of the agricultural South like an oasis; it was nicer than I pictured it in my mind. I have seen newer cities in the North try to emulate the rich historical markings that seemed to come naturally in this city, but this was the "real McCoy." Merging the new and the old, Selma was visually pleasant. A marking point for all of the smaller counties around it, Selma was our destination on the map, but Minters was farther away than we thought, and it wasn't even on the map. One day when I had time, I would like to come to Selma and gauge the true climate of this city, but not today. It was 1:45 p.m., and we had only forty-five minutes to make our destination. As we finished off two twelve-ounce Mountain Dews, we knew it was time to stop and ask someone for directions.

We were now nearing the place where we got our surname. This is where my grandparents met and married. My father, James, and his sisters, Lubertha and Juanita, were born here as well. I could only imagine what this place looked like in the early 1900s if it looked like it did now. Perhaps the old redwood in the field could tell the story better than I could. Perhaps the Alabama River that separated Selma from Dallas County could tell my story. They were witnesses of time, yet they did not speak. If they did, our plight would be easier.

Jim and I had spent more time together this weekend than we had in a long time and it was "all-good." For two kids that were at one time inseparable, sometimes we didn't see each other or talk for weeks. Jim was married with two kids; I understood that his dreams now involved more than himself and pursuing them took time and energy. To me, it was far more important that he finished what he started and be a good father and husband.

Ever since childhood, we have always been able to turn adversity into opportunity. During one cold, snowy December, Jim and I took the lemonade stand to new dimensions. We were headed down Seven Mile

Road for our paper route when we met, head-on, one of Detroit's famous potholes. We were in the Vega, a little hatchback Mom bought so we could get to school and she to work. When we hit it, it was the biggest jolt and loudest sound for a chuckhole I had ever experienced. Usually, when you hit a chuckhole, you usually say *"Darn!"* and keep going. This chuckhole was different, over a foot deep and warranted pulling over and surveying the damage.

When we got out, we noticed that the front right hubcap was gone. As we canvassed the area, we found other hubcaps as well as our own. Then we heard a loud *"Kaboom!"* as another car hit and its hubcap went flying off in our direction. Jim and I looked at each other and smiled, as we were thinking the same thing. We camped out and soon had the hatchback full of hubcaps. In the '70s, cars had hubcaps instead of chrome and aluminum wheels, so we kept busy during rush hour. When people stopped, we retrieved and gave them their hubcap, providing a service. When they didn't, we kept them, matched them, and made sets. Jim was actually waiting for Cadillacs and Lincolns to roll by because their hubcaps were more valuable.

We rushed to do our paper route, hoping no other enterprising kids would move in on our idea, then came back the same night. When it was all over, two days later, Jim and I had made over one hundred fifty dollars off hubcaps. The city finally fixed the pothole on the third day, probably because it was so bad. This was just the beginning of some of the capers we pulled off together. As we grew older, those capers became more intricate and demonstrated that working smart had its advantages over working hard. Being in the right place at the right time with the right idea had its rewards. This, however, was about as innocent as it got.

We were going deeper South, a place where it all started and where my grandfather and grandmother, Allen and Jessie Coleman, left long ago. This funeral took me to her side of the tree's branch, hopefully, shedding light on her side of the family. It seems the memory of my grandfather was more pervasive in my life; I recalled him saying and doing things much more clearly. He was a wise old man. I would, often times, try to mirror his likeness even when my father, his own son, came up short. I wondered what attracted my two grandparents, the handsome, brown-skinned man in the sailor suit and the woman that could pass for white after sunset.

I understood my Grandmother Jessie less, but when I viewed the land scarcely clad with houses, land that has made few changes in time, change to *only* land, trees, and sky as far as the eye could see, I had a clearer picture of what puzzled me. When I think of my grandmother, I remember the good and the bad. With all things considered though, the bad wasn't really so bad. When I think of from whence she came, I can understand better what once puzzled me. The deeper I probed, the more the pieces started to fit, although there were many. Her makeup was complex,

though in my youth, I rarely took any of this into consideration.
Why did she seem to show favoritism? I didn't know.
Why what came up came out? I didn't know.
Why did she often side with and encouraged the demise of a happy family? I didn't know.

I can only think, and sometimes I thought too much.

When I think about the old log cabin house that marked the beginning and end of my search, I see a little girl born in the hub of confusion almost a century ago. I could only imagine growing up in an environment where fear ruled and, at the same time, provided a shield of protection from harm. Set aside far beyond any thoroughfare of communication or knowledge, distant from any highway or byway to any populated place, and, strangely, foreign to neighboring counties or communities, this is where my grandmother was born, lived, and gave birth to my father.

In ancient Greece, the purpose of the woman was simple. Conquering the surrounding lands required a vast army to reign amongst any adversaries. The woman's duty was to reproduce, raise children, and provide manpower capable of maintaining the home front and conquering surrounding lands. Boys were trained to fight wars at an early age. This marked a time when males were accepted and women were rejected to the point where women and their female offspring were ostracized and even put to death. Success and failure was determined by the ability to produce what was needed.

Will Small, a wealthy, but unlearned man, probably knew little about ancient history. His world constituted a vast agricultural area no greater than twenty square miles. He ruled every inch of it like a Grecian warrior, leaving his mark and claiming all spoils until all was inventoried and accounted for. In his world, he owned the land and handpicked the occupants according to his criteria. In the post-slavery era of the late 1800s, this was all he knew. The son of slave owners knew that owning slaves was no longer accepted, and that he must use his land in some other way. What was he to do?

When I was a child about a year old, before my parents moved to the university, my parents lived with my grand-parents in a reddish-brown duplex style home owned by my Uncle Ted Coleman, a numbers man turned businessman. (Ted was my grandfather's first cousin, Dad's second cousin, and actually my third cousin. Since he was much older [closest to Dad's age], I always acknowledged him as an uncle since he was a role model for me. Ted never worked for anyone and was a successful man who owned motels and property, and was a numbers man. He used to give my grandfather large paper bags of money to put away.) Upon moving, we would still see our grandparents everyday when my parents had to work. As I drive down this street today, the neighborhood is nothing like I remembered as a child.

Although the house was still there, this once fully occupied street of well-kept homes has finally lost the war to drugs and urban decay. The corner store adjacent to the apartment building just two doors down where we would see pigs' feet in a jar submerged in vinegar water and say, "*Yuck*," was no longer there. Doc, Mrs. Coreen's live-in friend, the same old man who used to sit out on the front porch with his dog and provide us with hours of countless stories about the old South, no longer existed. The backyard where we played so freely between clotheslines, where I first smelled fresh-cut mint leaves, is now filled with old junk cars and scraps thereof. The early '60s were carefree. I was surrounded by people that loved me. If they didn't love me or if that love was in some way conditional, I was too young to know the difference. The world was my apple. This was long before education, achievement, surpassing my parents' expectations, and retirement came into play.

* * *

Grandparents' House. 444 E. Philadelphia St., Detroit, Michigan. 1962.

When I was a baby and my parents lived at my grandparents' house, my father's sister, Lubertha, came for a visit. My grandparents anticipated her arrival because they would see her newborn baby, Joy, for the first time. Lubertha's husband, Phillip, was in the service, stationed with his family. They drove from Wyoming to Detroit. Joy, a newborn only a month old, was about three months younger than I was.

Grandma had a way of meddling. She began a rumor stating that I was a bit darker than my father and brother, so "Kirk may not be James's son," according to her. She did not take into consideration that both my grandfathers, Allen Coleman and T. K. Lampkin, were darker than me! Mom was never away from home in Chicago, so this accusation was both demeaning and absurd.

As the car pulled up, Lubertha held Joy as Renee, her sister, tagged along as they all headed for the house. Renee was such a pretty girl. Grandma probably loved her more than any of us until DeMal came along. If Joy looked anything like Renee, she would have been satisfied. Joy was wrapped up like a gift; they could not wait to see her. When Grandma unveiled her little angel, she almost hit the ceiling.

"Oh, Lubertha! Why she haf' to be so black?!" Grandma said.

That was all my mother heard from upstairs. Dad looked on, angrily shaking his head.

"Momma, how can you call anybody black when yo' Momma black as soot?" Dad asked.

Granddaddy was at work. It was usually his job to keep grandma in her place. No one could quiet her like granddad. Since no one was there to contest her, my Dad stepped in. Jessie did not like that. She and Lubertha turned red with anger, although for two different reasons. Needless to say, despite all, Joy turned out to be a beautiful woman and her mother's most devoted child. Until I understood from whence she came, I could not love my grandmother for who she was. Although I believed there existed a formula to rise above any obstacle in history's shortcomings, there are some people who, instead, knock it down and tread it under their feet generation to generation.

Wisdom just does not always come with age. I have argued with some old folks who unsuccessfully tried to convince me of something I did not believe and would never believe. When wisdom does come with age, however, it is a wonderful thing to listen to a venerable old man or woman speak volumes, taking you to a place and time that is personally their own. It is the nectar that youth is deprived of today.

Nowadays, a grandmother could easily be forty-five years old, further perpetuating a cycle of "microwave existence." Having tried both the microwave and the good old-fashioned conventional oven, I admit that a bun in the oven tastes much better. It has a crispness that modern technology cannot duplicate. Although my grandmother was a very good cook who made the best flapjacks (pancakes) and cracklin' cornbread (cornbread with chunky pieces of bacon), she was not what I called wise, God bless her. She kept my wise old grandfather fed, and that was enough for me. It was an experience to see him put his fork down, add butter and Alaga syrup, and sop up any bread put before him using his hands.

There was something about the old man that made him special. Before I even knew who he was, I extended the utmost hospitality to him. When he came into my restaurant at the museum and I spoke to him, I decided then and there that he would never pay for lunch again, as long as I was under contract there. I was taken by the fact that this man, well over eighty years old, would ride the bus to the Museum of African-American History everyday, eat quietly, and leave so politely. I would see hundreds of people a day, but for some reason, I was drawn to the tall, frail man who had lines of age like those of an old oak tree. His curly, gray hair was tied into a ponytail, which seemed uncharacteristic for a man his age. I marveled at the peaceful nature that he possessed, along with his ability to function so well for his age. What was his secret?

    One day as I was at the cash register, our paths crossed. It was after the lunch crowd died down; there were just him and two tourists from Germany. People came as far away as downtown for our lunch special, which offered a choice of four entrees and two side dishes for five dollars. Beverages and desserts (like Kentucky Bourbon Pecan Pie and Key Lime pie), were extra. Although exhausted from the lunch crowd and involved with the kitchen staff working on a party, I talked with him anyway.

    "How are you, sir?" I asked.

    "I'm just fine, young man; thanks for asking," he said.

    "What would you like today?" I asked.

    "Oh, I think I'll have the smothered chicken with gravy," he replied.

    "What sides would you like?" I inquired.

    "I'd like the mashed potatoes with gravy and green beans. Are you the person responsible for all this good food?"

    "Yes, sir, you can say that," I replied.

"I think it is so nice that you have something like this in the museum. It is a blessing, and I look forward to it everyday," he said.

"You mean you come to the museum everyday?"

"Yes, if the weather and health permits. You see, my greatest joy is to sit in this beautiful restaurant, in this beautiful building and eat lunch here. This place is truly a treasure, and I want to thank you for your part in it."

"Do you live nearby, sir?" I asked, thinking he did.

"No. I stay about six miles away. I catch the bus here and walk from Woodward."

I was amazed that this old man had such a simple, yet amazing story behind him. Before I could think or measure any long-term cost analysis, I spoke, "Sir, I admire you. I really do. Anytime you come to this restaurant, you will eat for free."

"You know, I have no problem paying—it's ..."

"No, sir, I insist. If anyone asks, you are my personal guest."

"Thank you. This is truly a blessing. I have been blessed to meet so many who have been so nice to me," he said.

"So have I," I responded.

Shaking hands he said, "I'm Charles Dawson."

"Kirk Coleman, my pleasure."

If what I had some control over meant so much to this old gentleman, he could have free reign. When I think about waste and employee pilfering, why not feed the old man? What about the women who rubbed their breasts on me and sweet-talked me when they told me that they didn't have money for lunch? What about Chef Lenn's three-hundred-pound cashier who ate lunch before everyone else, then took home dinner to feed her whole family? I almost fired her for being nasty to Mr. Dawson. What about Chef Lenn who made money disappear at an alarming rate at the blackjack table? No one should have said anything about this man eating free, but they did, and it puzzled me. They knew not to say anything to Mr. Dawson. If they had, it would have warranted from me a reaction similar to Jesus' in the temple. No one could sway me away from something I felt so strongly about. No one dared.

Although he ate dinner and dessert free and often took something home, I am still indebted to him. This old gentleman became my friend. When I had time, I would sit with him, and he would talk about his life, taking me back years on a journey to a time I only read about in books. When I didn't have time, I would always, at least, acknowledge him and make sure he had everything he needed and make him feel at home. No matter how hectic things were for me, Mr. Dawson always had a kind word and was a lighthouse of wisdom and forethought. He was a walking testimony of what God could do with one who listened; he brought out the best in me.

What made Mr. Dawson so special was that he was there when I needed him most. When DeMal, a strong, presumably healthy young man, left for work and died mysteriously on the job a hundred miles away from home, we were sick with despair and in need of answers. The museum, the institute where I put my life on hold in order to manage it, provided no flowers, no cards, no visitation from staff, nothing but "sorry." That's okay. I didn't even notice at the time. My church, Hartford Baptist, was supportive though. They sent a deacon to the services, a gentleman whom I'll never forget. All my true friends like Jerry, Dwayne, and Mike were there, among others. Even Chef Lenn fed the family and visitors quite well. It was after the smoke cleared, two weeks later in the fall of 1997, that I realized that I must continue to live, despite the greatest loss in my life. Even so, my pain was deep, my stomach wrenched, and I could hear and feel my spirit scream *"Oh No!"* with each thought of what happened.

When I finally returned to work, there he was sitting in the same place, with his umbrella and newspaper rolled the same way. He radiated the same as before even though my vision was clouded. When I sat down and talked with him, I explained my absence. Someone had already told him what happened, and he expressed the greatest, sincerest words of sympathy I heard thus far. He told me not to question God and said he prayed for me all the time. I believed him. He then quoted a poem verbatim to my amazement:

> *Death is just a dream,' tis said*
> *Why then at the words 'He died'*
> *Tears of sadness start to flow*

And in mourning we will go?
Why the mourning?
Why the tears?
'Tis just the end of toiling years
Death, my friend, is just the door
From this life to evermore
When for God we daily live
And our service freely give
Why then should we sob and cry
At the thought that we must die
When our Lord was crucified?
Just remember how He died
Freely from His wounds He bled
Hear Him as these words He said:
'Thou art father, I am son, I am son
Not my will, but thine be done'
So if from death you would be free
And fearless you would love to be
Give your heart to God today
In it let Him have His way
Death you boldly then can face
Wrapped in God's abounding grace

When I heard the old wise man recite this poem in resplendent, romantic verse, I realized that this was his purpose. Some people believe in angels, but this one lived, breathed, and had a zip code. I asked him to write this poem down to give to my mother for I knew, not having the strength to attend her own son's funeral, she was still hurting deeply. Mr. Dawson came back the next day with the poem. I thanked him and asked him to call my mother and speak to her sometime. To this day they are good spiritual friends. This formula for wisdom needed to be sprinkled over the masses like autumn rain, but was of short supply and in far too little demand.

Chapter 10

It didn't take long to get from central Selma to its outskirts. We both agreed that we should stop soon for more directions while we were still in a populated area or risk talking to cherry trees, peach trees, or cornfields later on. We had little time left, and our map showed us very little. It was time to put our inherent communication skills to work because things were getting critical as far as time was concerned.

We were all good communicators—Jim, DeMal, and I—although I was probably quietest of the three. When I was with Jim or DeMal, sometimes they would see someone they knew and talk and talk until there was virtually nothing else to say. Perhaps the skill came from Dad. He was a radio dispatcher for the City of Detroit. He also used his gift of gab for manipulation and seduction. When I was young, a friend of his once told me Dad could "talk a hole in a woman's panties." Now I understand.

Perhaps the skill came from my mother because I have seen her cut people to shreds with surgical precision with or without cuss words while, at the same time, being loved and admired by people of all ages. For one that didn't talk much, I have never seen her without words, if needed. She just gets wiser with age, reading the Bible from cover to cover over and over again.

"An empty wagon makes the most noise," she would say, and I never wanted to be one.

"There are three guys over there," I said, pointing to the right.

"Yeah, one of them should know," Jim said.

We pulled into an auto repair shop that looked like a blast from the past. Oil was the substance that covered the floor. Tires and wheels were stacked in no particular order, and auto parts looked as if they were taken off years ago and left in the same spot.

An early '70s tow truck was the centerpiece of this portrait, probably a workhorse in its day. Today it looked as if it needed the services of the shop it probably once helped to build. Retirement for the old truck was imminent, but the old auto repair shop was the artery of its current existence, a relationship built on security, dependency, and need. How could one refuse the other?

Three men stood around under an awning, not wanting or needing to work on their tans. When we pulled up and waved them over, the older man came to the car. It was 2:10 p.m., and the clock was ticking. It was hot that day for April, even in the South. This was what I wanted though—the sun's rays. It was cold and rainy in Detroit and most of the way down. My body and spirit needed the sun. The harsh winter of 1998 took some of my color away, and I wanted it back. Besides, I wanted a head start on tanning season.

"Sir, do you know how to get to Minters?" I asked.

"Whad' you say?" he said in a slow Southern accent.

"Sir, do you know how to get to Minters?"

"You mean Minnoz?" he said.

"Yeah, Minnoz," I said, remembering how Dad said it.

I was somewhat embarrassed that I did not address this man on his own simple terms. A young lady from Virginia attending Spelman College once told me I was condescending; I didn't know what the word meant at the time. Before I gained some fluency in the language, I didn't think to take words apart and look at their meaning first. Webster's New Collegiate Dictionary defines *condescending* as "to descend to a less formal or dignified level," or "to waive privileges in rank." It also means "to patronize." Webster defines patron as "a person chosen, named, or honored as a special guardian, protector, or supporter." Did she mean, perhaps, I lived an ivory tower existence and came down or descended every now and then to "kick it" with peasants and underlings, people inferior to myself? My '63 bug, errant mattress spring, and working lifestyle should not have indicated that to her. If it did, I don't know how.

When considering the denotative meanings of the word, is *condescending* that bad anyway? When a businessman goes to an elementary school to talk to kids and plant dreams, what is that? When successful people with homes work in homeless shelters, what is that? Isn't faith itself structured on God doing the same thing, descending to a human existence some 2000 years ago? I would think that if you meet people on their own terms or "level," it is a sign of respect. If you meet them at their own level and respectfully bring them up to yours, it is a sign of grace.

On the other hand, if you'd much rather, like an ostrich, bury your not so pretty head in the sand of doubt and denial, only to come up for reinforcement among your peers, this is not wise. A lion waits in the marsh. As you drink from the mouth of the river because your long legs equip you to do so and because you are able to, life goes on for other animals as well. As you greedily gorge yourself at the mouth of the river, you hate the fact that water escapes you and trickles down the river behind you. You think that if somehow you could fashion your bill to ingest the whole river, you could solve this dilemma—no, stop it!

Unknown to you, a crocodile slowly swims against the current in your direction.

Kirk Coleman

He hasn't eaten since the teenage antelope he snagged last week, with the exception of a few fish. What was used to your advantage is now working against you.

The sixteen-foot crocodile has identified your strong birdish odor as he closes in within 20 yards, 19, 18, and 17.... He already knows how you taste, your level of resistance, and kill time—all of your needed stats. As you drink from the mouth of the river, the only sounds you hear are your own. As you guzzle and slurp and come up for air, you see movement in the water coming in your direction. Then suddenly your fight or flight protocol kicks in, but you realize it is too late to fight, so you bolt. Blindness and greed appear to be your tragic flaws with equally tragic results. *Oh shit!* you think, as the croc makes his final move whether you see him or not.

If you only stayed on the shore, you could have quenched your thirst just the same. You wanted more than nature's allowance. Now the only thing that remains between you and dry land is a sixteen-foot African crocodile. Although you've never been eaten before, you know it would hurt, and you probably won't make it home for dinner yourself, if this creature had its way.

Then in a last-ditch attempt to survive, you remember that you are a bird with smaller wings and bigger legs than most. You spring up and out of the water, just missing the jaws of the crocodile by inches. You jump better than you fly, so this episode is not quite over because you are coming down on the croc's back. You run down his back and find a pathway to safety as you quickly make it to shore.

Your comrades are with you as you celebrate and do a victory dance. *You may be an ugly bird, but you are not dumb like that old crocodile,* you think. You and the other birds run up to the bank and provoke the old crocodile that, although hungry, must find dinner somewhere else.

All of this excitement made you thirsty again. As you cautiously walk up to the shore to drink, this time you realize how marvelous you look in the water's reflection. It took adversity for you to realize that you are the smartest and prettiest creature in the jungle. You will immediately start breeding to create a "super nation" of birds just like yourself. Besides, after what you went through, you owe yourself some fun tonight. You are a hero, and this is your day.

You convince the other birds that drinking from the mouth of the river is better, and "if we all drink at the same time, we could make the river dry up." As you march away to your habitat, high on yourself, you suddenly feel like you've been hit by a 720-pound "can of asswhoop" that caught you off guard. It is the lion ... the lion in the marsh. Didn't you hear the narrator say the lion *waited*? Did you forget? He didn't forget you .... He was there the whole time.

He uses his teeth to tear into your throat. He cuts your air off as you swing like a cheap rag doll in his grasp. Suddenly out of haste or clumsiness, the lion bites through your long rubbery neck, severing your head completely. It falls into the sand and watches the rapture. In a cloud of dust, your awkward body is slammed to the ground by an oversized cat, like a ball of yarn, while your eyes are blinking at a distance. Where are your comrades now, you try to think?

    You try to die, but for some reason, you just can't. It happened all so fast, all within the course of thirteen seconds. The lion rips open your body, eats only your heart, then drinks the water you made such a fuss about. Come to find out, he was thirsty, but he didn't want to get wet.

SINZ OF THE FATHA

Chapter 11

The fruits of my labor were starting to pay off as I was selected by the brewery where I worked for a week's vacation in Hawaii for having the highest brand numbers in the state of Michigan, giving me a taste of the good life unknown to most twenty-eight year olds. There is a saying in Hawaii that people who visit are "newlywed or nearly dead"; I was neither. I convinced Chyna to come with me with a little persuasion. After all, this was a once in a lifetime trip.

"Let's take the honeymoon now and get married later, since the honeymoon is free," I said.

She consented although she and I were not married. She knew I was going anyway, so she finally decided to go.

Going to Hawaii, Waikiki, and Honolulu on the big island of Oahu in 1991 spoiled me. The warm, coral-filled waters and sun-soaked sands had me counting the days and living a life of luaus and leisure while I fell in love with Chyna, the girl of my dreams. After ambling up the white sands and wading in the azure waters, I pondered the thought of being a beach bum there, living off pineapples and sunshine, as opposed to being a working stiff in Detroit. My attitude changed, as one who was fortunate enough to see the beam of light, but returned to live in darkness. As the days went by, ever so swiftly, I had to think of the plane trip back and the life I left behind in Detroit, to my dismay. Ironically, I came back and was laid off from my job two months later.

After being exiled from Detroit's beer industry, I knew I had to do something more productive. I could have gone to a competitor and taken a similar position, but I was burnt out. It was an uncomfortable feeling sitting in church Sunday, knowing that I sold alcohol all week, like a mercenary who doubled as an altar boy.

Since I was laid off, rather unfairly, I broke the code. I took my employer to court, because, despite everything else I went through, his last words to me were, "We value some people more than others."

My last words to him were, "See you at the crossroads."

After all the smoke cleared and all of the information, records, statistics, and depositions were presented, my attorney was confident that I was too convincing of a client, and this case would never appear in court.

"Kirkwood, you never cease to amaze me; you are the best client I ever had. You have a brilliant mind. They won't stand a chance against you in court, especially with these records we subpoenaed," my Jewish attorney Schwartz said.

"Am I your best client because I did more work than any of your clients, attorney?" I asked sarcastically.

"Hell, no, Kirkwood; you still have to be an attorney," he barked with a grin. "You just felt so strongly that these people put shit on you that you took control."

"Yeah, controlled anger is a serious thing. I could have just lost it and gone into a rage, but that's what I felt they wanted."

There were many days and nights when I was at the law office or at home working on my laptop, preparing, and responding to discoveries. The attorney first approached my case with skepticism. When all of the facts were presented (and there were many), he understood why I felt I had been discriminated against. It was elementary. We built a friendship out of adversity that continues to this day and have lunch from time to time. This was good, because I never liked fair-weather friends.

"Before I start teaching at Ferndale, I need a job, Attorney Schwartz."

"Sure, Kirkwood. I could use an investigator to interview some of my clients and gather facts before I talk to them," he replied.

"Sounds good. I'll talk to you when I get back from New York. By the way, I need eighteen hundred dollars."

"When?" he asked.

"Now," I said.

"Oh, Kirkwood. The check hasn't cleared yet!" he said.

"Attorney, this is a drop in the bucket of my award," I quipped, "and it's been four business days."

"Okay, what about twelve hundred?"

"Okay," I resigned, knowing I'd get the rest later.

"When you come back, we'll go to the bank and transfer the rest into a new account," he added.

"Okay, attorney, sounds good. I'll get you something nice to put in your office from New York."

"Good! Every time I see it, I'll think of Kirkwood Coleman, the fighter for justice and equality, *and* the best client I ever had."

That's my Jewish attorney and friend, I thought. I got him a souvenir when I went to "The Big Apple." I could not think of anything more appropriate than a figurine of the Statue of Liberty—one for him and one for me.

* * *

When Mrs. Berry, the principal, walked into the suburban elementary school classroom that was predominantly white, but diverse with blacks, Latinos, and Filipinos, she was shocked to see the quiet scene before her. The classroom was silent and the children were working on their assignments as though they were on a mission. Acting as if they were in a library, the third graders did not say a word, but silently acknowledged Mrs. Berry. I was quietly sitting at the desk, looking over the lesson plan.

"Mr. Coleman, how long have you been with Ferndale?" the principal asked.

"Since 1994, going on about five years total, but I left for a year and a half for a business venture."

"I can tell you have been around by the way the kids are acting. You know, this is one of the less manageable classes in the school," she said, looking puzzled while surveying the room.

"Really? I think they are little angels."

"You're kidding. Most subs would have lost it in here."

"Really! Some teachers are too high strung when it really isn't necessary. If you look at the blackboard, you might find the answer to your question."

As she went to the board, she read the reason the kids were so quiet:

Write 25 times if disruptive:

We, the students of Washington Elementary, understand the importance of treating everyone with the utmost respect. This is especially true for visiting teachers because our goal is to exemplify the true meaning of education and make our school proud. In doing so, we can create an ideal educational environment for ourselves, while building a pathway for the future.

Mrs. Berry smiled and came back to the desk. "Could we request that you come to our school more often, Mr. Coleman?"

"Well ... ah ... usually I prefer to work at the high school. I just opted to work here because nothing else was available today."

I would not tell her the real reason. It was too idealistic, too chauvinistic, and, perhaps, the reason so few men are in elementary schools today. *I would not inflict my views on her today*, I thought, even though I felt comfortable with her. Elementary school teaching is a woman's forte, but this is part of the problem as well. There are few men who will accept the challenge today. Since so many families are dysfunctional and Ritalin is the drug of choice, more and more responsibility is put on the teacher to fill a growing void. In elementary school, especially the lower grades, I would find myself wiping runny noses and going home sick myself. When a little girl in second grade jumped in my lap, I knew then that I needed more distance from the kids. A teacher's job is underrated and underpaid, to say the least. I preferred secondary education because the kids, at least, gave me the space that I required, and they made their most vital decisions near graduation. This is what I felt but chose to keep to myself. If I wanted to change the world, however, this would be a great place to start.

"You say you have a business. What type?"

"I cater and do concessions management," I replied. "In the summer, I also have a small landscape design business that trims bushes, small trees, and builds ponds. I started small with both, but had to hire a few people to meet the demand," I replied, hoping she didn't mind if I were industrious.

"How long have you been doing that?" she asked.

"When I lost my job in private industry in the early '90s, I had to eat, so I started doing my own thing."

"I'm glad you're here, Mr. Coleman. The schools need more people who have other things going on, but the problem is they are too busy doing other things. I hope you come back again."

"Thanks," I replied.

I would always joke to myself that President Coolidge was turning over in his grave concerning the thought that this middle school was named after him. I wondered if the school was built over some toxic waste site, and if the kids were some kind of experiment in hyperactivity. The reality was quite different though. This area consisted of low- to middle-class transient whites and some minorities, including Latinos and Filipinos. Ferndale was not the posh suburb of metro Detroit, just another caricature of an imperfect world. I was only on a mission to give something back and put my degree to use until I had had enough or witnessed some results. I did not know which would come first.

In this school system, the students welcomed me. There were some teachers and administrators that were rude and didn't even speak to me. I knew that Ferndale was changing. In fact, it had changed a lot from what it used to be. I was glad to be a part of it all. Besides, I always felt that some who chose the field of education had some difficulty communicating with adults. I was cognizant that I was a minority in this environment, but this time, I knew what to expect.

Don't make waves. Keep your mouth shut is what I had to keep telling myself.

It worked.

It was not by prejudice that I concluded that a more radical means of education was needed, such as "shock treatment" in secondary education. It was through experience. Kids thought the age of forty was extremely old; this was about the average age of a teacher. Some kids couldn't relate, wouldn't listen, and failed to learn. When an elderly, white, sixty-year-old female teacher asked a black sixteen-year-old student what he wanted to be, his response was, "A pimp. Can I pimp you?" The student was expelled, and the teacher herself took leave. This was a signal that the changing rural school system needed people like me.

I remember in 1998, when a six year old brought a gun to school near Flint, Michigan. He shot and killed a little girl. What happened to the angels? Only God knows why the boy had to be black and the girl white. The little boy, so young, was demonized by two generations of instability, guns, and illegal drugs. The little girl's family was not interested in these perplexities.

Before the "A" could be in apple or the "B" could be in boy, the "O" first must be in order. Rural schools were changing because many people were now given an opportunity to live where they pleased. The influx of the students exceeded the demand for a diverse staff, in some cases, creating communication barriers and issues. The inner city schools had problems of their own. State legislators have taken control of the urban school systems, such as Detroit, further creating a wedge between education and race. Were the kids failing the system or was the system failing them?

When I walked into Coolidge Middle School, I noticed how hyperactive the kids were. The smell of industrial cleanser, chalk, and everything that resembled a school permeated my senses in the old, brick school. The ringing of the bell was loud and irritating, signaling the kids to come inside. The hallway was bustling with activity. Some ran and some walked as a student darted by me, slapped another student on the back of the head, then ran. I went to the office to get my assignment for the day.

"Good morning."

"Ah, good morning, Mr. Coleman. You are in for whom?"

"Mr. Pitkoff, I believe."

"Good! You have alternative education today. Here are the keys. Have a good day."

In retrospect, there was something sinister about how she said what she said. I knew that I was in for a challenge because alternative education had some of the less manageable students, those emotionally impaired, mentally impaired, as well as Ritalin pill poppers. Alternative education was a roundup of "problem" students and students with problems in order to attempt to teach them skills they needed to succeed. It also removed problem students from normal classes so the other kids could learn. This was part of my challenge because the teacher absence rate was higher among these classes; I can see why.

When the bell rang and class started, I noticed that some of the students looked older than usual for eighth grade. Most of them looked like they just woke up, put on baggy pants and jerseys, and came to school with little or no preparation. A few of the boys seemed out of place for my idea of an eighth grader. Later, I found out some of them had failed. The initial exchanges I had with them were professional, but that didn't last too long. Three particular boys ran together and claimed to be the tough guys in some sort of gang. One was an interracial young man (probably black and white), the second one black, and the third one looked to be a corn-fed Jethro-type white young man. I remember what the old folks used to say, as I was prone to listen to them: "When you see a black and white together, either they're looking for trouble or they're the police." These guys were definitely not the police.

Willie Brown, the mixed student, was the toughest and slickest student in the school, although he wasn't that big. He stayed in trouble because he was not your regular eighth grader. He was like an old '70s pimp in a kid's body—although without the green leather suit. His name came up when some audio-visual equipment in school turned up missing. He also had run-ins with the law outside school. Although I didn't disclose much about myself, he and his friends tried to size me up. He made it clear that he was the "top dog," and the other boys followed his lead.

Kirk Coleman

"Mr. Coleman, are you from Detroit?"

"Yes."

"Were you ever in a gang?"

"No, not really."

"Have you ever smoked weed?"

"No. What does that have to do with you?" I asked.

So I lied, but in teaching sometimes, things are better left unsaid.

They must have tried to gauge how much we had in common.

"Get back to your assignment," I said sharply.

It was only a one-page handout. I knew there wasn't much to do in this situation except to try to establish control and to baby-sit. All of the tools and paint were put away. I proceeded to put on a tape of Forrest Gump. The troops were getting restless.

When the assistant principal, Mr. Csebian, walked in, I noticed how much he looked like the actor Jeff Goldblum.

"If you have any problems with these guys, send them to me immediately," he said.

As he was leaving, he stared one of the students down while another came from behind, grabbed him, and locked his arms at his sides.

Not the assistant principal, I thought.

Two other kids got up laughing, ready to assist in the assault.

"Let me go. Let me go ... I'm serious," Mr. Csebian said, struggling on his way out.

As the corn-fed young man held the principal defenseless, Willie got up with his fists balled up, smiling and shouting, while circling him.

"Now what! Now what!" he shouted, acting like he was going to punch him as he was being held.

These kids were beating up Mr. Csebian, the assistant principal, and I could not believe it! When they let him go, he adjusted his shirt and left quietly. Was this the person I would send unruly students to? If I kept any order in this classroom, I knew I would have to apply alternative measures.

"Mr. Coleman, can you beat up Mr. Csebian?" Willie asked.

"We beat up the head principal before, and we beat up Mr. Csebian the other day, real bad."

"We had him pinned on the table. He could not get up until we let him up," another student said.

I knew this question was coming, and I knew the answer, but chose to skirt the issue.

"Our gang is tough. We don't bow down to no one. When we put a hit on you, it's over," said Willie.

I smiled. I was actually starting to enjoy this conversation because, alarming as these remarks were, this was what most kids talked about. It gave me the opportunity to do what I did best and show these kids that they were only ... well ... kids. They brought me here, but I would bring them back on my terms.

"You guys are suburban gangsters, aye? Have you guys ever been in the city with this gang stuff?"

"No."

"I didn't think so. Have you guys ever heard of a street called Fenkell?"

"Yeah," said Willie.

The other kids didn't know.

"I tell you what. If you guys are as tough as you say, let me drop you off around Fenkell about 3 a.m. If you are lucky, you'll still be running at 8 a.m. If not, you didn't run fast enough. Come on, guys, I'll drop you off."

Their eyes were as big as saucers, as though I was sitting by the campfire telling a ghost story. They were scared, yet they wanted to know more about this place they had never been. It was their choice to be suburban gangsters or real ones.

"Are there many gangs on Fenkell, Mr. Coleman?"

"There are some, but the biggest threat is a lone gunman who approaches you at random when you least expect it and robs you at gunpoint. Since you are the only witness, and he doesn't want to get caught, he'll probably just shoot you on G P."

"What's 'G P?'"

"General principle—for the hell of it. If you don't have anything on you, he'll just get angry and shoot "General principle—for the hell of it. If you don't have anything on you, he'll just get angry and shoot you, but if you do, he will want to make sure you won't tell anybody so he can get away. Are you guys ready to watch the tape?"

"Yeah ... uh ... yes, sir."

I won. I knew I should not have gone there, but I did. In hostile environments, I've learned to take victories any way they come.

Chapter 12

We drove over the historical bridge of Selma. The directions given to us were sketchy and warranted us stopping again. The man at the shop said to drive four to five miles until we got to a highway and turn. I watched the odometer while Jim drove what seemed to be ten miles. When we drove past seven miles, I got nervous.

"Maybe the old boy was talking about country miles," I muttered.

In the course of an eight-mile route, we had only passed one service station, a closed-up building, and nothing but red dirt and pine-laden landscape. When we approached a neat wooden building made from finely sanded logs, we stopped. It fit in so well with the background of pine trees, some peaking at sixty feet. Brick or stone could not master the same effect as the pine log building with a background of pine trees. It was a product of its own environment and a landmark in unadulterated simplicity. *Thoreau might have written an essay on this pine wonder*, I thought. I would not. This would soon become our lighthouse, setting us back on course.

When I walked up the strong, squeak-proof steps of the well-manicured log building, it looked to be some type of restaurant and country convenience store for the elite. It smelled of fresh pine, a scent that aroused my senses. Inside of the store, the floor, ceiling, and walls were much of the same—richly manicured pine. There were two men sitting inside the store, playing cards. They both were white, one with brown overalls and the other with a neat plaid shirt.

Another man with an apron, clean-cut and professional looking, came from the back with some baby back ribs that he put in the heated display.

"Sir, do you know, Willie Small?" I asked.

"Sure do."

"I'm trying to get to his funeral today somewhere in Minters. Do you know the church where it's being held?"

"Yeah, just drive about four miles up this road to Highway 14. When you get there, veer off to the left to Highway 11. Take that about three miles 'till you get to Highway 5. You should see a church on the left after a couple of miles."

"Thanks. Just let me write that down. This highway to 14. Take 14 to Highway 11."

"Yeah."

"Three miles to Highway 5."

"Yeah."

"Then about two miles to the church?"

"You got it," he said.

"Sir, how far away is the church from here?" I asked.

"About eight miles," he said, cutting the ribs in the heated display.

Shit, I thought, *I hope they ain't talkin' country miles.*

I spoke up. "By the way, this is a beautiful store you have here."

"Thanks," he said.

I went back to the car with the directions, and we sped off. We were getting close to missing the whole purpose of the trip. If they closed the casket, and I didn't get to see him, we would fail to fit the pieces together in this puzzle. I had to see him with my own eyes. I had to look at his hands, the structure of his body, the length of his face, and his bone structure. If they closed the casket, a door would close linking us to the past, the present, and shutting out the future. If they closed the casket, I should have never left Detroit, and this whole thing would remain a mystery. My eyes were the judge and the jury. What was transferred through any other medium would have little or no value.

As we raced through Dallas County, Alabama, this time I didn't notice the sharp disparity of the rich and poor. This time, the "shotgun" homes, as they called them, didn't vie for my attention. I have seen them before, elevated above ground, where a dog, cat, or storage could exist anonymously. Sixty-five yards away, I didn't notice a large, well-kept mansion that needed paint. I didn't wonder how two extremes could live together in such close proximity. I didn't think about the beautiful pine log store that we passed and didn't wonder if the people in the "shotgun" homes were allowed to do business there. Perhaps the people in the "shotgun" homes were like me—they didn't notice at all. I, personally, would find it hard to live in a place that had such a bearing on my ancestors, while at the same time said, "Don't worry, be happy." It was like falling victim to "Three Card Molly" twice.

To anyone unfamiliar with the game of Three Card Molly, it was practiced, as I know it, on the bus lines of Detroit. It looked easy, but it was a scam. Most people got taken in by it at least once. It usually took place in the back of the bus, out of view of the driver. Optimism and hope were the first reaction to the game, soon replaced with anger and regret. It happened to me once going from high school, but only once.

When the crowded, noisy bus coming from downtown was making its way towards Detroit's outskirts,

Kirk Coleman

people napped, read, and chattered—the usual. We were just getting off Ponchatrain, making the stretch down Seven Mile Road. I noticed a guy two seats over who pulled out three cards, shuffled them, and asked if anyone could guess where the ace of diamonds was. That looked easy, and besides, there were only three cards. Then he spoke to me.

"Come on, man, find the ace of diamonds," he said to me.

I carefully watched as he moved his hands, putting one card over and under the other, keeping my eye on what I thought to be the ace of diamonds. When he stopped, he put the three cards down atop a briefcase.

"Pick the ace of diamonds," he said to me.

I immediately went to the card I had been following and turned it over, looking for the ace of diamonds. I found it.

"You won! This time, try it for money."

"Nah," I said, knowing I only had eight dollars in my pocket.

"Who wants to try; it's an easy game. I'll double the pot if I lose."

"I will," a man said about four seats down as he pulled out a ten dollar bill.

After thirty seconds of shuffling, the dealer laid the cards down. The man picked up a card, turned it over, and it was the ace of diamonds!

"Damn, you won," the dealer said, paying the man twenty from a large roll of bills.

Maybe this wasn't a scam, I thought. If the other man could win, then I knew I had a chance myself. I knew if I could double my money, I could eat at Checker Grille that week and still get to and from school and work at the clothing store. *If he asks me again, I'll bet five*, I thought. He did.

"I'm doubling bets. How much you got?"

"Five," I said.

"Anyone else to get in on this?"

"Yeah, I have five," another man said.

"Okay, when I finish shuffling, y'all just pick a card that you think is the ace, but you got to pick at the same time, okay?"

"Okay," we agreed.

I watched his hands shuffle, as this time they moved faster than before. As he laid the three cards down on the briefcase, I picked a card that was in the middle and the other man did the same. When the dealer turned it over, it was not the ace of diamonds.

"Dealer wins—pay up," he said.

Flipping all the cards over, he showed that the ace of diamonds was, in fact, there. It was just where I least expected it, proving that his hand was quicker than my eye.

When he added our money to his roll, I thought about the luxury of eating at Checker that just slipped through my hands, but it didn't bother me much. What got me was that when he got off the bus, the man who won twenty dollars earlier got off at the following stop with a sneaky grin on his face. As I looked back, they

Kirk Coleman

both crossed the street, probably to catch the next bus in the other direction. They were in cahoots, and I got hoodwinked as a result of it. I would never play this game again.

"By the time you lived a full life, you would have received three educations: one from living, one from going to school, and one from sitting and watching the world go by," Mother once said.

This was a lesson learned on a Detroit bus.

There was a time when I thought I was all grown up. When I was a child, I couldn't wait to grow older, thinking that the world would open up once I got to a certain age in my teens, and it did to a degree. A flask of knowledge would flow and things would be better with age. I thought I was a prisoner as a child, but I didn't know then that a child was free to dream without restriction. As you grow, thus comes the walls of intervention, with complexity. Who then is the prisoner?

Long before kids learn how to drive, there is a game that they play called "that's mine." It is especially popular with young boys. The object of the game is to say "that's mine" before other kids do when you see a car driving down the street. Then you win. It was that simple and could be done with real estate as well. We took it a step further and played "that's yours," another way we played "the dozens." It never really mattered that we didn't get to keep the car, drive it, or "floss" with it. It was all kid fun. We knew one day we could afford it on a fireman's salary. After all, isn't that what most kids wanted to be?

When you do finally learn to drive and get your first car, it is usually a hand-me-down, certainly not the shiny new car you picked. It may be the same model of car, but your car is likely to be twelve years old and blowing smoke. You change the oil, hoping it will get you through high school and to work at your part-time job at the supermarket.

You decide that although being a fireman is "way cool," and you'd only work ten days a month, you couldn't overcome your fear of heights. When you tried to rescue the neighborhood cat from the tree during childhood fireman maneuvers, others had to rescue you as well. You also find that you are allergic to cats, just like your dad. That's okay. You'll just go to college and be somebody ... else. You will get that car and anything you want when you finish college. In just a few years, you will be able to say, "that's mine." In the meantime, just borrow your dad's car for the prom. He drives a Lincoln.

A lot of time has passed since you saw it and laid claim to that dream car. You are an adult now. The razor and shaving cream that you once used for entertainment now has purpose. By the way, they still make that dream car you wanted as a child. It comes in a few models now, only faster, sleeker, and brighter than ever. The night before you go to the dealer, you contemplate, as only adults do. You want to live your dream. There are, however, a few things you must take into consideration:

The student loans that you owe are equivalent to the GNP of a small country in South America.

Kirk Coleman

This is your first job since waiting tables in college, and you really don't like it.

Your bosses don't seem to like you either.

The test came back positive, so you might need to look at a minivan.

Insurance rates are 20 percent higher in the city; you live in the city.

So on ....

So forth ....

You go to bed, wondering why you were cursed with a fear of heights in the first place.

The next day, something conveniently comes up more important than what you planned the night before. As you pull up to the stoplight, your dream car pulls up beside you, only to remind you of the appointment you missed. You look over and nod at the driver in admiration because it's only right. You could have looked the other way. He appears to be in his late fifties. He nods back. When he pulls off, you smile and think to yourself, "that's yours."

Chapter 13

As we covered the last remaining miles, I chose to meditate, preparing myself for what was in store, hoping it would all register with clarity. It was so much easier to digest death when the body failed over time and gave some warning, even though it was still sad. Whenever I looked around at Woodlawn Cemetery and saw DeMal's headstone, as well as others surrounding it, it just seemed as if he should not have been where he was. His neighbors lived their three score and ten years, that is, seventy years, while he, at twenty-six, barely scored. He didn't even take risks that some took that sent them to an early death. He did not live recklessly and make the necessary adjustments when time draws nigh, as some do. He did not live to see his son graduate from, or much less, start school. Despite all, the medical field assured me his cause of death was "natural." That is what I found hardest to digest. After all, what was natural about a six-foot-four, twenty-six-year-old man dying without warning ... or was there a natural reason?

When Hank Gathers, a basketball player for Loyola Marymount University, played, I knew he was a promising athlete that would soon turn pro. He was a natural for the sport—slim and almost seven feet tall. During a nationally-televised game, Gathers clutched his chest, fainted, and never regained consciousness. Even though I never met this young man, his death saddened me. I thought of E. A. Housman's poem called *To an Athlete Dying Young*. In the poem, a young athlete, once the symbol of strength and agility, was carried to his final resting place. His records of accomplishment were complete; he would forever remain a hero. He was immortal, free from negative media-driven publicity, free from drug and prostitution stings, free from aging and deteriorating, and free from the influences of instant wealth. His loved ones, however, are in no mood for these perplexities. It is noble to remember young athletes for their dreams, as well as their accomplishments and eternalize both, because when you are young, your dreams are your reality.

Kirk Coleman

After following the directions given by the man in the pine store, we still could not find the church. I was starting to sweat, despite the artificially cool climate of the Acura's interior. If I had a choice, I'd rather be lost in the city than the openness of the country. In the country, there were no cab drivers to ask directions. There were no pedestrians. There were no landmarks. We frantically retraced our route, looking for mistakes. Failure was starting to appear as reality. We knew that once the casket closed, it would never open again for anyone. It was 2:30 p.m. We were late with good reason. The landscape, once beautiful and tranquil, was now our adversary. The southern weeping willows resembled a group of Medusas, their long slender branches looked like snakes. The flora looked like pollinated ragweed, and the fauna were like gray rats, certainly not black ones, with long pink tails. I hated them as if they were evil. I hated them because they turned against us and stood in our way as a silent partner in time's assault.

Even Jim did not know what to do, so he kept driving, hoping we would stumble upon an opportunity. I truly believed in opportunities. It is favor that leads to progress. I also believed that to whom much is given, much is expected. Opportunity is much like a talent. If you manage it unwisely, you lose it as well. To hoard it is unwise. If you ignore it, it will pass. However, if you share it, you can live up to it.

It just puzzled me how I attended a seminar on problems in the workplace with people from all over

Michigan and yet, the greatest concern seemed to be affirmative action. When I looked around the room of about forty people, thirty of them were white males. Seven were white females. There were four black women. I was the only black male there. When I looked at my watch's digital reading, it said 1999, so I was in the right place in time. I only wondered if they would have been satisfied if only half or a quarter of me was there? I wouldn't have reacted as I did, but the rebel-roused response of the people there incensed me. I stepped into the ring.

[Introduction] "Last, but certainly not least, in the far left corner representing the endangered species of the free world, weighing two hundred forty pounds ... Kirkwood Coleman!"

The crowd roared, but not for me.

When the bell rang, I danced around and punched them with the diplomacy of Dubois. They stalled and staggered, only to punch back with force, staggering me as well. Seeing that this was not going to be easy, I threw a McKay punch to let them know he was there, and I wasn't having it. I had too many experiences in this ring and would rather be carried out than fold.

I jabbed. They stumbled.

I returned with the objectivity of Douglas and the eloquence of Cullen when I had them on the ropes, not wanting to hurt them too bad.

They were bleeders.

When the bell rang everyone seemed exhausted, and I was the lone wolf that caused a near riot. Even the black women who tried to silence me were told to stay out of it. This was my fight. As I walked out, people looked at me differently and the security presence seemed to increase. There is certainly a historical wedge between people of different races in the workplace that cuts hard and deep. Some think the wedge isn't enough. Some think the wedge is too much, while some, like me, believe it shouldn't be there at all. Although I didn't have the answer to the problem, I knew that one existed. I'm not sure if we solved anything this day, but I got a few things off my chest. I may have won that round, but there was no reason to celebrate. The fight is more than just one round. The sport is, at times, unscrupulous, and the judges make the final decision.

    In Detroit, people gather for the Eastern Market Annual Flower Sale during spring. Eastern Market is a gem for Detroit, known for its freshly-cut meats, produce, and specialty items. The market attracts people who live in Detroit and its suburbs, giving Detroit the opportunity to shine. This is one of the few times that make Detroit look like a thriving multicultural city it could be. Detroit is changing for the better though. Our stadiums, football, and baseball teams are new and back in the city. Business, industry, and residences are relocating to Detroit; even tour buses are visible.

    I credit Mayor Dennis Archer for his diplomatic style and "olive branch" approach. He welcomed anyone and everyone to make Detroit work, but was criticized for "selling out" to whites and major corporations. Despite my numerous experiences in this arena, that is not how I feel. Anyone who has traveled to Chicago, New York, or Atlanta knows that it takes more than one race or nationality to build a great city. Detroit, rich with cultures, is a Mexican town, a Greek town, and a Pole town. Metro Detroit has the highest population of Arab Americans in the United States per capita and has all the markings of a cultural Mecca. Detroit is predominantly African American though, and this is what most people see with one eye closed.

As opportunity presents itself, people in Detroit fear being shut out from Detroit's own rebirth. People expect their quality of life to improve, and they should. Even I know that when *they* come, they come in mob capacity, and they come in force. Historically, *they* have a way of making you feel you don't belong in your own home. *They* manipulate the women while sheltering their own. *They* cause the greatest traffic jams and make catching a cab even more challenging. I still welcome them.

I think people are wiser now since the riots of the '60s. I hope so. With exception to the auto industry, Detroit is years behind most major cities because of mismanaged opportunities. The city once burned, people died, and it was left as a symbol of urban blight. As a reminder of what happened years ago, Detroit annually burns in a "devil's night" (the night before Halloween) ritual as photographers from all over the world watch as both frustrated landowners and mischievous teens burn blighted property. Mayor

Kirk Coleman

Archer challenged the residents of the city to take control of their lives, to take back the city. Then the eyes of the world closed on Detroit's demise. Its citizens and the churches were the true leaders of this revival, as well as business and industry, so all must share the wealth. Although the mask takes on many faces, not all will tolerate it if they recognize it. Many people fall into this category. The game of possum will not work.

While engaging in barbershop debate, an often unavoidable ritual that all men endure, I found that some were skeptical about Detroit's rebirth with good reason. Shoptalk enabled men and women to listen and engage in conversations of local, national, and world proportion, providing opportunities to respond with their own views. It was an opinionated discussion of current events with no referees; everyone seemed to have an opinion.

Some people, I found, would much rather see tumbleweeds rolling down Woodward Avenue, Detroit's main thoroughfare, than accept the coming changes. Some believed the next mayor would be white, that Detroit was part of an intentional urban restructuring plan to skyrocket property value. Some believed Wayne Williams did not kill twenty-eight people. Some believed the Tuskegee experiment fell far short of its estimated target. Some believed that the Jesus portrayed in pictures would not have survived such an arid climate, and that Moses did not look like Charleston Heston. Some believed that blacks would again be shut out of the lion's share of wealth in Detroit's revival.

My views were radical for this day, in this place, because I supported changes despite what was said by my stylist, Roger, and his clientele. The new Baseball Park had opened that week; construction of the football stadium was in progress. I disagreed and held my ground. My challenge to all that didn't agree with me was to think of something that they did best. Go downtown and start a business on paper. Work on legitimizing your business, and then put your name in the hat. If you loved what you did and did it well enough, it should flourish. If it did not, then ask questions. If the questions were not answered, get serious. If you were ignored, then and only then did you have the right to get angry, but only after self-examination. It worked for me. Once you got in, don't forget to bring others in with you because otherwise you will not just fail, but you will be known and remembered as "the spook who sat by the door."

Like the Berlin Wall, I just wanted the barriers to fall *sometime* during my lifetime. If I did not, I would be no better than a stone-throwing, graffiti-wielding racist that tormented a black or Jewish family in the suburbs. Despite my faults, I always thought I was above that.

It was the strangest animal that I have ever seen as a child. It wobbled as it walked along the back fence, moving away from detection. It was a big, fat, rodent-type animal, but too big for a rat. I called my

Kirk Coleman

father who happened to be home that day working in the garage.

"Dad, Dad, there's an animal on the fence," I whispered excitedly.

He came out of the garage and looked around the corner.

"Damn, a possum!" he said.

He ran back in the garage and grabbed a shovel, then approached it with caution. The possum tried to dodge him, but had no place to run. Dad swung the shovel, hit the possum, and the possum lay there lifeless. He scooped the animal up in the shovel and threw him in the garage wondering what to do with it.

He called a friend from work who hunted and ate possum. He knew his family wouldn't take part in this debauchery. When the friend showed up, the possum woke up and took on a whole new persona. He fought with every bit of energy he had like a wolverine— one of the fiercest animals, pound for pound. Somehow, the little possum must have known he was to become a link in some barbaric, unorthodox food chain. Perhaps he knew that if he continued to sleep, he would end up in a pot with potatoes and carrots.

They approached.
He charged fiercely.
They stepped back.
On and on it went.

I looked around the corner and watched excitedly, letting the men handle this fight. They cornered him cautiously, boxing him in as he fiercely fought the whole way.

It appears that a sleeping possum is just a deception. Pound for pound, it is an extremely vicious animal that uses sleep to lull its adversaries to a false sense of perception. It resorts to whatever it takes for survival when it senses danger—whatever works. As a child in the South, Dad found out the hard way. A possum that he thought was asleep fiercely bit him. Whenever I see the strange little animals today, I just watch them go their own way. I have too much respect for the species to interrupt, and I have a profound appreciation for wildlife. Besides, animals imitate human life in the strangest ways.

Chapter 14

In the marketplace, growers come from all over the area to sell their plants and flowers at premium prices. They have been preparing for months, nurturing a seed, caring for, and protecting the plant for this big day. Growers want to have the best plants because consumers have many choices. They could buy elsewhere if the harvest were subpar, and the price above market prices. This is an opportunity for growers to ask and receive the highest yield for their products, but competition is tough. The consumer is meticulous. He could go elsewhere to avoid imperfections or price gouging. The market has its own built-in system of checks and balances. In this case, a begonia is not a begonia when there are so many others.

Take, for instance, a grower who is having difficulty keeping good employees. That is how he tells the story. He will not tell of mismanaged funds or bounced payroll checks. He avoids mentioning the tyrannical environment that his employees must endure.

The seeds grow.

He will not speak of his glass-ceiling policy or his prescribed intentions to limit his employees to only one aspect of his business so that they will not even think of starting their own. He flinches when he considers even the thought that they might talk to each other or an outside vendor for fear his name will come up in the conversation. He sabotages the work environment with minefields in order that people feel powerless and never see their personal worth.

The seeds grow.

A young man just recently took a job with the seedy grower. It was just two months before the flower sale. The young man, fresh out of college with a degree in horticulture and chemistry, had dreams of becoming a master grower. When the old grower found out, he swallowed the bitter pill of envy. He went home that night and dreamed that the young man was his competitor in the marketplace, and his flowers were more robust than his own were. He then decided to show the young man how hard this business could be. Instead of seeding, growing, and maintaining the plants, the grower had the young man loading and unloading trucks. He gave the duty of plant maintenance to a sixteen-year-old high school student. One day the student didn't show up and the plants were wilting, so the young man, although busy loading trucks, watered them and moved the low-light plants out the sun. His initiative angered the old grower.

"Wha'chu try to be—a boss, kid? Don'a u think. I think. Leav'a the thinking to me. Just you load'a the truck!" he barked.

The seeds grow.

Just one week before the big flower sale, the plants were at their fullest bloom. The marigolds were robust and reaching for the sun. The salvias were sensational and bountiful, and the geraniums were genuinely gorgeous. In one more week the grower would reap the rewards of a full harvest. This week, however, he would jet down to Key West for some deep-sea fishing with his friends. Last year, he had an eighty-pound Marlin on the line that got away; he would use 100-pound weight line this time. He would allow no room for error. He gave the orders for the week and threatened to fire the sixteen year old if he missed work again.

The sixteen-year-old student feared the old man so much that he didn't dare tell him about the school dance he wanted to attend that weekend. He just procrastinated as teens do, thinking it would work itself out. The day before, he found out the girl Daisy who made his hormones go haywire would be at the dance. He knew that if he did not show up for work that day, he might as well not come back. He contemplated the night before, as most teens do—job or hormones, job or hormones ....

He never showed up again.

The sun was hot that weekend, as you might imagine. The heat made wavy lines that rose up from the ground to the sky. The flowers cried out, but there was no answer. A grayish cloud formation covered the sun for a while, only to give way to the sun's ample rays. The low-light plants begged to be taken out of the sun. No one answered. The heat was intense; finally, the cries of the plants turned to whispers that would soon fade to white.

The rains came, bringing back to life each plant on the brink of death. It was as if heaven opened and gave them more than what was needed. The plants, on the brink of annihilation, were coming back to life as the water resurrected them, drop by drop. If the water was coming from heaven, then God was holding a hose. It couldn't be him. God should be loading and unloading trucks. It was the young man who could have taught the old grower a bitter lesson, but why didn't he? Why did he neglect his duties and do exactly what he was told not to do? The narrator loves plant life too much to give the old man what he truly deserved.

While driving with the predisposition that we failed, we stumbled onto an old dusty road. It diagonally fed off into the highway and divided the thick forestry on each side. It appeared least traveled of all the roads I've ever seen before in any populated area. In fact, we were not even sure it was a road. Jim pulled up and looked to see if it ended anywhere in the distance. It didn't. Jim backed up and carefully drove up the road, hoping to find something. We knew that the road meant little as an end. What we were looking for could be off the road or miles back because in the old South, it was a luxury to live on the populated roads, a luxury that people of color did not have. The land beyond the roads was rich with agriculture and allowed the poorest of the poor survival, despite the cruelest socio-economic climate. Figs, mulberry trees, Chinaberry trees, grapes, wild melon patches, and wild game kept many from starvation, people who had nothing but the land.

 My cousin Chuck once told me the story of how he and his brothers, thirty years ago, would leave in the morning in search of dinner. They didn't go to a bank or the store, as some do now. They didn't go shopping or swipe an encoded plastic card at a register, then walk out with groceries. They didn't write a check. Their store was the rich, fertile landscape of the South which provided a harvest once so bountiful that multitudes of people's destinies were altered as a result of it.

 One day they came upon a Chinaberry tree, where robin redbreasts would feed off the tree and would be so drunk on its fruit that they would literally fall off the tree. It was entertainment for the boys, watching the birds get tipsy, argue, and fight with each other before they blanked out on the rich liqueur of the tree's juices, like relatives at a family reunion. Chuck and his two brothers would throw the intoxicated birds in pillowcases and take them to their mother where she would perform culinary miracles with the least amount of supplies in the cupboard.

When she finally called them in for dinner, they had smothered robin redbreasts, rice, brown gravy, and biscuits. I can remember sampling such delicacies as quail, ostrich, swordfish, and even buffalo, but never robin. A mother's innovation must have started here in the South.

Considering the delicate mixture of what we were looking for, we started at the roads and were prepared to go miles inward, into the backwoods, if necessary. Darkness and depth were, again, linked as the night. While slowly driving up the road, the terrain changed for the worse. Bumps and potholes were getting closer to one another, and the trees were threatening as they hovered over the roof of our sports sedan. Jim slowed down and suggested turning back. He had just washed his car hours before. We really should have been in a truck.

Suddenly, out of nowhere it came—humming and sputtering, as if it ran on fewer cylinders than was required. In a cloud of red dust, we could see a little red car maneuvering up the road, like it knew where each and every bump lay. We were glad to see it though. We had not seen anyone for minutes, which seemed like hours in our search—a simple thing we, as Northerners, took for granted everyday. Like being on a deserted island far away from civilization. Although rich in fertile agriculture, we still lacked what we needed. If not but for the moment, now I saw why it existed, and why other people were so important outside the abundant island.

"So, this is where Southern hospitality comes from, people or the lack of them?" I gathered. It is the same reason that people in New York walk past each other without notice. A distinct hospitality that the South claims to be different from anywhere else is with reason. It is a hospitality the South claims as its very own.

We were prepared, however, to exchange some true Southern hospitality if necessary. We needed information and had the approaching vehicle just where we wanted them. They could not pass unless they came through us. The narrow, bumpy road warranted that we would meet, regardless of intent. If we were ships, this road was a canal; the captains would, at least, wave.

The little dusty red car slowed and pulled up as we made room on the narrow road and opened the window. In the car was a black middle-aged man in his late twenties. In the car also were his wife or girlfriend and a little child. Wherever they lived must have been somewhere up the road, and I could imagine how it looked by observing the state of the road. It didn't matter though. They were rich, and we were beggars at this point.

"How y'a-doin'? We're looking for a funeral for Willie Small," I started. "Do you know 'em?"

"Yeah," he replied.

"Do you know where it is—the funeral?"

"Yeah, 'sat a church 'bout a mile an a ha'f fum heah," the man said.

Jim interjected, "Can you take us there?"

The man paused, but only for a second.

"Shore, jus' foll'a me."

As we turned around in the narrow road to follow them, I looked at Jim and nudged him with my elbow.

"Good idea, bro."

"Yeah, I'm tired of asking for directions. It's about time to get Missouri up in here," he said.

I immediately knew what he meant. Missouri's state's motto, "Show Me," expresses the need for action over talk. If not for the oral tradition that helped me visualize a time I did not live or experience as an adult, I wouldn't be where I was now. Without the language, I would certainly not be this far. Now was the time for action, to see for myself, and put some paint on the picture, providing some dimension, if possible. Now we knew we would at least get to the church. It was more than just solving the missing pieces of a cross-generational puzzle. It was mere respect, family supporting family in a time of need; we wanted to be there.

As we followed the little car for what appeared to be the shortest trip of our journey, we were excited for what was to come. It was rather embarrassing to come so close and miss our mark, but considering where we came from and where we were, it was not so bad. We logged over eight hundred miles that weekend in April in 1999, and that was just one-way. Anything could have happened to set us off course, but it didn't. Being lost is just a diversion that stirs the senses if you are found.

I remember when DeMal walked off at a zoo when he was a toddler; we looked for minutes, but it seemed like hours. When we found him, we wanted to kill him and hug him at the same time; we decided to hug him. We feared losing him and did not let him out of our sight again the whole day.

Being lost made us look at things differently as well. Aside from conveying an array of emotions and getting weary from it, we gained a sense of appreciation for being where we were. Is it an inherent quality of the human psyche that we must lose something first *before* it has value? I struggled with this often.

When my first girlfriend came to visit me in Atlanta, she took a bus ride from Northern Michigan University for twenty-four hours to stay for ten days. I had been celibate for months and was tired of Marzell blazing me for "not getting any" during my first year of college. If it was any consolation, I went on dates and did make the honor roll that first year. As for Marz, he got some, all right, picking up a gorgeous girl in his ballet class at Spelman, although I thought he was studying engineering. An ex-jock, I could picture him in his tights and ballet slippers at six foot two, weighing 230 pounds, surrounded by delicate women half his size; it wasn't a pretty sight. He knew where to find them though, and he was rather smooth with the "balls of a brass-ass monkey," as the old folks used to say. Who would have thought of taking ballet?

When Anna came to visit Atlanta, I picked her up at the bus station, eager to make up for lost time. I was going to peel her like a banana when she got back to my apartment with her high yellow self. When I helped her put her luggage away, I hugged her from behind, about to kiss her neck, when I noticed the red blemish. I almost lost it.

"What is that on your neck? Is that a hickey?"

"You can say that, but it's not what you think."

"Hold on! Back up! Leave your shit where it is. *Don't unpack shit!*"

"But listen, Kirk ...."

"Listen, my ass! You mean you came all the way to Atlanta with a hickey on your yellow-ass neck? I'm putting you on the next bus back, bitch!" I said, reaching for the phone.

"I know you're mad, and I don't blame you, but please listen to me! If you send me back, I'll go, but let me explain before you decide," she said tearfully.

"Okay. Explain a hickey on your yellow-ass neck."

"A guy did it"

"No shit!"

"A guy did it out of spite, a guy I go to school with. He did it because he knew I was going to Atlanta to see you. He knew I loved you, and he did it to make you mad."

"You made me mad, not him. He's an opportunist. It's you. You also disappointed me. You let me down. All that."

I paused, rubbing my temples.

Kirk Coleman

"Listen. I need to be alone. Stay down here for a while. Watch television or whatever. I have a headache. I'm going upstairs to lie down."

"I'm so sorry I disappointed you, Kirk."

"Yeah."

As fair as she was, how could I not notice a hickey on the side of her neck? I could see it from ten yards away, once I knew it was there. She had an explanation though. On the bus twenty-four hours, she had enough time to rehearse any scenario. I had to punish her though, because what she did wasn't right. But for some reason, I wanted her then and there. How could she let him come so close? Although I was a man and she was a woman, and there was a bed in close proximity, our relationship, once valued, felt cheapened.

When I awoke later that evening, she was asleep in my bed, wearing her gown with her arms around me. Little did she know that her time was short. Little did she know that the future consisted of only the ten days she would stay with me and nothing more. Little did she know that her file was deleted from the hard drive and was only running on disk.

I didn't send her home prematurely. She stayed, and we almost fell in love again, although I knew it was just physical. My first love would not be my last. By the way, add one skeleton.

Although my second flame went to Spelman while I went to Morehouse, there were a few before her. We did not meet on campus, but at a club far away uptown. I was drawn to her aloofness, her innocence, her black Shirley Temple locks and pretty feet that I noticed through her sandals. I asked her to dance. She said, "Yes."

"Hi. I'm Kirk. What's your name?"

"Hah you doin'? I'm Lena," she said in a sweet Southern accent.

Taking her hand and caressing her palm I said, "The pleasure is mine."

Until the lights came on, we continued dancing and virtually closed the club.

I was not so innocent; my dark side was developing. The magnetism I felt for her increased when I pulled her closer during a slow song. She knew what I was thinking then and there. I wasn't looking for a wife this night; I never went out with that intention, but she was a keeper. I kissed her on the cheek, walked her to her car, took her number, and made plans to see her again.

For our first date, we went to the beach on Lake Lanier, forty miles outside of Atlanta. Going to the beach gave us the opportunity to see each other more closely, with fewer clothes than before. The sun radiated off her olive complexion and illuminated her Indian-like features. I was attracted to her like a magnet. She was a natural beauty who wore very little make-up and had the prettiest hands and feet I had seen on a woman thus far. We put suntan lotion on each other and went into the water. We went deeper and deeper until the water covered our waists. We kissed. I pulled her closer and closer. We were almost one in the water. She surrendered her tongue, and we kissed, only stopping to come up for air.

When we came out of the water, she looked down, blushed, and said, "Oops!" Not knowing what she meant, I looked down and quickly adjusted my trunks.

"Oops!"

I didn't intend to show her as much, so I blushed as well. She became my girlfriend soon after that day in '83 at the beach.

When we were apart, we would talk for hours on the telephone. Two weeks into our relationship, as we were talking one night, the operator interrupted the line.

"Emergency phone call from Derrick. Do you accept?"

"No," she replied.

The operator hung up.

"Sorry about that."

"Yeah. So who is Derrick?" I asked.

"He's a friend I use to go out with a while back," she replied.

"So what's the emergency?"

"Probably nothing," she said in a Southern accent.

I told myself to leave it alone, although that word "friend" had a dubious affect on me when it came from a woman's mouth. I was turning into a skeptic with reason. Then the operator came back on the line.

"You have an emergency call from Derrick. Do you accept?"

I was livid even though I didn't know her long enough to share my anger with her. I thought it best to just wait it out and survey the situation.

"No," she replied.

"Yes, we ... uh, she accepts," I said.

"I wanna' talk to you," she protested.

"No. Listen, you need to talk to Derrick now, because what he thinks and what you tell me don't match up. It's not fair to him, and it's not fair to me, so handle it the best way you know how. I'm going to bed—bye."

"Okay," she said almost sadly.

As I lay in bed, I stared at the ceiling, wondering why the monkey wrench kept appearing more often than not. I was becoming a stoic through life's experiences. I wondered how Derrick must have felt because, regardless of what Lena said, I knew she left him for me. If nothing is fair in love and war, as they said, I should have felt victorious. I just didn't. I wondered if this situation would, someday, put me in Derrick's shoes. Considering the male ego, this was where no man wanted to be.

Our attraction for each other superseded the obstacles we encountered during the first two weeks. As we progressed, we became closer with each passing day. She and her family opened up to me and became my family away from home. She became part of my own family, venturing as far as Detroit, whenever I returned home to visit. We became fixtures in each other's lives. Five years went by; it was nearing the time to step up to the next phase of our relationship; I questioned myself if I was ready. I had to decide if I wanted to live permanently in Atlanta, as Lena expected me to. I knew that after dating five years, some people who viewed our relationship from the outside would assign me the title of "jerk," but my intentions were honest, and I loved Lena. Time went by so fast. There is something about dating five years that doesn't sit too well with women, their family, and friends, especially in the South. There is an old saying, "Why buy the cow if you can get the milk for free?" It was time for me to "put up or shut up," which meant commitment or "letting the cow go free." Now I had to decide. However, looking at the situation back home, there were a few things I had to consider: Dad was gone, and Jim and his wife were moving out, getting their own home.

Around this time, I found out that DeMal was skipping high school. Jim took him to school, watched him go out the back door, and followed him to a video arcade down the street. Mom was recovering from hip replacement surgery, and I knew she needed me, although she was too independent to ask.

In '88, I made some critical decisions that changed my direction and destiny. At the time, I was a relief man for an Atlanta-based Miller Brewing Company distributor, building and selling displays, merchandising, and driving large beer trucks. It was a very good job with good benefits. However, I resigned this job when Atlanta hosted the Democratic National Convention, and I was given the opportunity to take on a supervisory position in food service. I thought it was a good opportunity at the time. After a year at the Miller company, I quit that good job to partake in a large-scale food service venture that lasted only a week because I thought it would look good on my resume, giving me future opportunities of similar caliber. The ghosts of my fine dining past were forever haunting me or was it just control? I always knew there was something out there better for me. I just didn't know exactly what it was.

During that same year in 1988, the heat in Atlanta was fierce. One Sunday I was up, showered, and decided to go to church. I had a narrow escape on a motorcycle with a negligent motorist earlier that week. I knew I missed danger by mere seconds—if that. Fortunately, I was unscathed. I was grateful to the force that saved me. Whatever it was, I knew it was greater than me. It was too close to forget. Had the accident happened, the outcome would have been ugly. I thought about that all week.

I remembered a church called New Salem Baptist Church that I passed in Southwest Atlanta while riding on my motorcycle. While traveling through my old neighborhood in West End, I noticed the large church hidden with little announcement in an area of middle-class homes. As the congregation let out, I noticed how young and vibrant the congregation of black folks looked. When I stopped to allow traffic to exit the driveway, I looked to my left and saw a young lady that immediately commanded my attention. As she walked to her car in her clinging attire, she knew my eyes were on her. She looked up, smiled, nodded, and went about her way. I smiled through my helmet, nodded, and pulled off slowly, thinking, *Goodness gracious.*

Kirk Coleman

I decided to visit New Salem one morning, two weeks after sighting the lovely young lady. Although I visited many churches, there was something special about this one. When I walked through the brass-handled wooden doors, the cool air hit me and dried the sweat off my body immediately. The feeling was matchless, and this time I decided not leave early before the service ended. I would stay until the benediction was pronounced. After all the singing and praises, the gold offering tray finally came my way. I gave gladly, thinking that someone had to help pay the electric bill. The church was nearly new, full of amenities, and was a sanctuary from the searing Atlanta sun.

When the preacher, Jasper Williams Jr., came out, I noticed what a showman he was. His deep, powerful voice roared in harmony with the choir. He sang "Amazing Grace," a song I learned word for word long ago while attending church with my grandfather, Allen Coleman. I sang along. The preacher was a rather stately, yet flamboyant-looking man, wearing expensive red, big block lizard or gator shoes that I could see from the back pew. I found that bright, flashy lizards were his trademarks in red, blue, maroon, or gold, worn to complement his suits and ties. Sometimes I would find myself guessing which lizards he would have on next according to rotation. I didn't care how flashy he dressed because he did keep the air on full blast. He had a flair that was befitting for his age—mid-forty.

When the preacher spoke, it was obvious that he came from a family of preachers active in the struggles of many. He was a wise man under siege by life's obscurities, and I could relate to him. He was honest about his own shortcomings. He was real and down-to-earth for such a distinguished-looking man. If I was the preacher, I would have been like him. I was satisfied and came back to hear him speak many times until I had had enough.

One day during the fall of '88, I told myself when the preacher asked people to join the church, I would join. The guilt of knowing I was a permanent visitor in a house I loved was finally taking its toll. Going to Catholic services with Lena didn't service my needs. I doubted I could ever become Catholic like she wished. I needed to hear from someone like me, who could identify with me.

"Father, forgive me for I have sinned," just didn't get it for me. I needed a breath of fresh air. When I joined the church, Reverend Williams came up to me and put his arm around me. I knew he was going to welcome me, and he did. What he asked me afterwards stunned me and almost knocked me off my square.

"Has anybody ever told you that you are gonna be a preacher?" he asked before the crowded church.

I looked at him, and if that look said anything, it said, "Are you serious, man?"

I was not studying theology. Besides, at twenty-eight, I was living too fast, often at warp speed, to consider such a commitment.

I looked at him, shook my head, and said, "No, sir ... no."

I didn't feel worthy, but I wondered what would make such an insightful man say something like that to me.

Before I knew it, I was baptized. As the water washed over me in the baptismal, I was not overtaken by a strange force that made me shake, gyrate, and quiver. I didn't clinch my fists and raise my arms to the heavens and shout "Hallelujah!" The water felt good though—and I was at peace, for a while. From this day on, what could I take with me, and what should I leave behind? Will my prayers reach higher than the ceiling now? Is God watching, and what does He think about all of this? Will He watch me closer than before?

Oh ... I'm gonna have to clean house—my own, I thought.

Within a few weeks I was active in the church's organizations and speaking to the congregation (somewhat nervously). I was on my way, possibly, to fulfilling the goals Preacher Williams set before me, and I was satisfied with my endeavors. I never saw the young lady again in clinging attire though. If I did, I would have definitely noticed. Was she an angel?

Meanwhile back at the ranch, so to speak, things were falling apart between Lena and me, as if we were trying to disassemble them ourselves. I was changing and so was she. It seemed as though once I looked at my inner self, my relationship and friendship with her spun out of control. Women always claim they want a God-fearing, religious man, but I beg to differ. Up to a point, my experiences suggested that women wanted an urban-warrior type—a roughneck, humble to few, and apologetic only to the female species. To a point, I gave them what they asked.

Perhaps Lena saw a side of me that she had never seen before. I was more spiritual, more compassionate, and less physical, while she seemed to grow more perplexed. I understand her though. We were young adults and made mistakes as adults do; guilt was probably taking its toll. She was Catholic and some of the things we did are not allowed in the Catholic Church—period. She probably looked at me as a catalyst in her actions. Why should she embrace my changes that year (and there were many), when my very existence changed her life? After all, I knew Derrick loved her. Would they still be together had it not been for me—happily married? Was I responsible for all of this?

Many times she knelt at the confession booth and said those words to the white man inside. There were many times she said those words with my face in her mind's eye. There were times, probably, that my name was on her tongue, yet restrained, and her breath was my own. So close we were, even her scent was my very own.

"Father, forgive me for I have sinned," should have been plural. Now the catalyst was doing some soul-searching of his own. Why should Lena even care? If we married and raised a family, we could have fixed this problem—love without commitment, but it all happened so fast. Other weddings came, and she actually did catch the bouquet, as bridesmaids do, while I leisurely moved to the garter, not really wanting to be there. When it all came to a head, and I knew she was restless and weakening towards other men's advances, I had to decide if I was leaving or staying with the person I loved in the city, the person I loved at the expense of my real family. When we talked about it, she would go cold and call me a "Momma's boy." One day when I called and knew she was home, the telephone kept ringing and ringing ... and ringing. In early 1989 I left Atlanta to relocate to Detroit. I left quietly, almost anonymously, not wanting to interrupt her life again.

Chapter 15

We could now see the church within the distance. As our guide slowed and pointed to the little church in the field, we pulled over alongside the vehicle and thanked him. I also graciously slapped his hand with five dollars and hoped it was enough. The church was forty yards off the road on a modestly sloped hill that faded into a backdrop of pines and weeping willows. The architecture was simple and non-threatening, unlike a massive cathedral or an urban church that must expand to keep up with a growing membership. It welcomed us warmly with the tradition of Southern hospitality, while exuding a simplicity that seemed timeless. The door was open.

This quaint, simple little church had a wealth of history behind it. Built in the early 1900s when churches were the nucleus of a community, this church had withstood many people's struggles, both black and white. It was once the anchor of this little community, servicing the needs of its citizens from education to matrimony, and finally, to death. My grandparents, Allen and Jessie Coleman, were married and baptized here. My dad went to elementary school here under the watchful eye of Willie Small, his grandfather. The same church hosted the funerals of those who did not migrate to Birmingham, Selma, or further north. It was the same church then as it is now although four generations have passed.

I could tell by the scarcity of parking places that we were late, and the services had already started. We parked on the grass like the others (there was no parking lot). Jim and I got out and rushed through a maze of automobiles, hoping that the people standing outside were doing so to get some fresh air or to smoke.

It just couldn't be over, I thought. As we walked up the concrete stairs, we walked past two middle-aged white men in suits standing in the door.

They must be funeral directors, I thought.

The suited white men and I nodded at each other as Jim and I walked in. I could see the casket right in the middle where the long aisle ended in the simple, architecturally-challenged church. The casket was still open! I was so relieved that the mounted tension from this journey fell free like a suit of armor. Thank God for "C. P." time! This time, it was in my favor.

I approached with tunnel vision, assuming Jim was with me, beside me, but I was not really sure. I didn't look around to see if even Dad was there with any other members of our clan. I looked only at *him* until I stood above *him* and kept my eyes on *him* the whole time. The door to the past began to open.

It was not that I had never seen this man before. This was my grandmother, Jessie Small's, brother. I had seen him at least twice in either Minters or Detroit. There was a picture in the family photo album with him standing in front of the old log cabin house when he was about fifty years old.

William Small Jr., or "Uncle Willie," as Dad called him, outlived his brother, Monroe, and my grandmother, Jessie. They all lived a long time, into their mid-eighties. My great-grandfather's other children from other mistresses were spread within a twenty-mile radius, but these three siblings had the same mother. *There were others*, I thought, *who were my grand-mother's biological sisters, born of the same parents*. It wasn't until recently that I knew the whole story. My grandmother has a half-sister, Carrie, who looks just like her, but was born of a different mother. In fact, they look like twins.

When I was young I didn't understand how families could "connect" through the seeds of the father without the womb of the mother. The womb is the centerpiece linking all with the same consistency as the others. All that develops from it has a common origin and a common purpose. For a while, this was all I knew. I always felt that the traditional family was linked by the mother's womb rather the father's pursuits. If a man ventured to other women, only his seed linked the offspring. As far as I could see in Minters, this was my dad's family's tradition—romance without commitment. Call it lust. The old folks called it the kettle of confusion. Despite all, this took place years ago in what is now called the Bible Belt. Can you imagine that?

    I carefully examined the man who lay there as if he were sleeping. Even in death, he looked good for a man his age. When I saw the large-framed man lying there, I could not help but think of my late brother DeMal. The hands were large, and the fingers were long, possibly double-jointed like DeMal's. The face was long, bony, and sculpted with little softness from fat, even with aging, like DeMal's face. The body, like DeMal's, was large and once towered well over six feet tall. He was fair-skinned with reddish-brown hair like DeMal. He was a natural for the sport of basketball, although I doubt he ever played. The similarities were profound.

    At that time Willie Small, the deceased, his father, my late great-grandfather, and DeMal, my late brother, were all somehow linked as one. I could see the transgression of my great-grandfather's genes in three generations, in three men, just as I imagined.

    That white man had some strong genes, I thought.

Kirk Coleman

I could see from pictures of my great-grandfather that he was white—pure white. If Emma, his mistress, was "as black as soot," as my Dad said, how come all of the offspring were so fair-skinned and appeared closer to white? How could my grandmother's "sister," Carrie, from a different mother, look like her twin? I wrestled with these questions as I viewed the lifeless body before me.

When I finally had enough and took in all my eyes could see, I took a mental photograph of my late Uncle Willie, the last of my great-grandparent's children I knew, just to make sure I could draw on it later. I then turned around to see whom I could recognize in the church and to look for my father.

There were a few seats left in the small church, but it was too hot to squeeze in, so we headed for the back. I scanned the crowd, looking around, nodding hello to people I knew. I could relax now because we accomplished what we set out to do and everything turned out well. We made it to the funeral, and I compared my Uncle Willie, my grandmother's brother, to DeMal. This was the reason we journeyed almost eight hundred miles to attend the funeral. This was the final piece of the puzzle that I needed to make sense of in this whole matter. With the puzzle intact, I could retrace history from the late 1800s to the present and find out, among other things, why my baby brother died of what the doctors called "Marfan's syndrome," a rare condition that hid under the veil of normalcy. Why did all indicators of this mystery point to Minters, where my inheritance started? Is this another part of the confusion that the "color line" brings? If so, I always thought the mask was surely enough for someone like me to endure.

* * *

When Dad saw us, he came to life. I noted he was proud to see us, recognizing we logged almost eight hundred miles to pay respect to his mother's brother. He was always proud of us, although at a distance. I just never felt the closeness to Dad that the other boys on the block seemed to share with their fathers. It seemed that whatever distractions he had, they took him far away from home even when he was present. Sometimes I have pleasant memories of him. Sometimes when I think of him, my memory is unclear, like trying to remember a dream the night before—only bits and pieces. Sometimes I'd rather not think at all about some of my childhood experiences.

DeMal, only a child, often put my very own childhood thoughts into words when he said, "I wish I had a Dad like Mr. Brown or Mr. Bridges," two fathers on our block. He didn't feel complete without a father at home. He didn't understand it was time for Dad to leave. He was too young. A child's eyes could never see that this was not how a family should be. Dad was rarely home, and when he was, the tension was as thick as a Tennessee fog. The lion and the cubs could no longer live in the same habitat. The lion had to leave before something terrible happened. It was bound to.

Perhaps Jim, the oldest, knew better than I that it was time. No one knew better than my mother that it was time. We all knew she was too good for what happened to her.

"Be careful what you ask for in prayer, son," she said. "If you don't know, just ask that God's will be done. God knows better than you what you really need. When I was young, I asked God for a husband, and that's just what I got. The only mistake I made was not specifying what kind. I should have asked for one who put God first and family second."

We knew we had to save what was left of our family at risk of the weakest member. The four of us, Mom, Jim, DeMal, and myself, would sit at the dinner table and talk everyday Mom was off work. "We are a family, and we love each other, and we are going to make it," she said.

DeMal, just a baby, didn't understand then and tried to hold on to what wasn't really there. Little did he suspect, at three years old, that he had a half-brother from another mother who was just being born and who would pass for his twin. History was repeating itself.

In ancient times, a man was highly regarded to have sons. Even today, it is a blessing to carry on the family name and legacy. It is a man's curse, however, to have three sons who love the woman he mistreated. As the father gets older and the sons mature, a system of checks and balances is created. The father not only has to answer to the mother, but also to the sons as well. Although a husband's and wife's relationship is personal, when the family unit falters, someone must step in.

As we matured from boys to young men, my parents were at the brink of separation in their marriage. DeMal was only an infant. He processed more turbulent data than he probably knew how to file at the time. Jim and I were much older; we had each other, although Jim adjusted better than I did. We were just waiting for it to end. We helped raise DeMal as best we could, although we were not his father. We were only kids ourselves.

In 1979 I took a day off from high school to accompany my mother to court to finalize her divorce. I met her downtown at work. We caught the bus to the courthouse while Dad drove separately. Dad sat in the same row as we did. I did not even speak to him. If I ever hated him, it was on that day. There was nothing now to stop him from carrying out this confusing family cycle. We, by no means, could let him make it our own. It was final.

* * *

As Dad stood there lighting up a cigarette, his hands were shaking as he adjusted the flame to the tip. His thin legs seemed frail now as he leaned on the church's entrance for stability, revealing his balding head. Dad was, for some reason, showing his age today. His legs, like DeMal's, were long and skinny with small calves. They would almost meet at the knees if he relaxed them enough. DeMal and Dad both had small hips and a very small ass. It was never a question that DeMal was his son, and that the two looked better in pants, opposed to shorts. I inherited my dad's ass, and that wasn't much, although I know there's more to it than just that.

Dad looked exhausted as he loosened his tie. He dragged on a cigarette and spoke to us with his next breath.

"So ... you all made it. I didn't think you guys were coming this far in so little time, but I'm glad you did," Dad said.

"Yeah, we decided to make the trip, but we have to leave tomorrow morning—Sunday—for home," Jim explained.

"Say, Dad, who else is here?" I asked.

"Willie C., Clarence Moorer, Aileen, Aunt Carrie ...."

"Aunt Carrie is here? Where is she?" I asked excitedly.

"She's in the church. You'll see her. Come on, I want you to meet your white ainty and uncles."

"Did Carrie bring her son with her? Hey Jim, what was his name? It must have been twenty-five years since we seen them in Pensacola."

"His name is Terrance," Jim replied.

"Yeah, he's here?"

"Yeah. He has a lil' girl and a wife. They're here," Dad said.

The casket was closing and the services were ending. The last sobs of grief were cried for the deceased, then it was all over. People started pouring out of the little church and congregated outside. Dad introduced them to us as they walked by, both old and new faces. We shook hands and hugged relatives to the point that I started getting tired. Perhaps it was the hot, searing Alabama sun coming down like a sledgehammer on my back.

It was mid-afternoon and the heat was starting to make wavy lines that rose up to the sky, something I noticed first in the South. Perhaps I was coming down off of all of the exhaustion and excitement of the journey we took. It was 3:30 p.m. Central Time. We were in Detroit only twenty-four hours ago. Although Jim did most of the driving, I was still weary.

The casket closed. As the procession moved towards the open, awaiting earth twenty yards outside, people spilled out of the church. Being from the North, I expected the remains to be whisked away to a cemetery for burial a car ride away. We didn't notice that the cemetery and church shared the same plot of land. A canopy, no more than twenty yards away, marked the final resting place where the last rites would occur. As we approached, I noticed the headstones. Each had a pinkish-reddish hue with dates on some going back into the early 1900s. The red clay-like dirt of the South was evident in anything concrete-based—highways, buildings, etc. Unlike Detroit, there was red dirt as far as the eye could see.

There was something peculiarly surreal about the whole scene that took my mind away to a Stephen King novel. The old archaic, rustic cemetery with headstones of a pinkish-reddish hue fading into a backdrop of weeping willow trees made this scene look

Kirk Coleman

like no other I have witnessed. The blurry, heat-induced lines made the backdrop even more eerie. This scenery once petrified me when I was a child, causing me to sleep in my mother's room.

Years have passed and although I am still observant, the observation does not lead to fear. My grandfather, Allen Coleman, used to say, "Dead people can't hurt you. It is the living ones you should fear." This makes more sense to me now than it ever did as a child. Growing up and obtaining the wisdom that separates a child from an adult is, at best, a luxury that all are not privileged to enjoy. A majority of wisdom comes from listening to the accounts of others, as well as from personal experiences. That, after all, was the mystery of and motivation for our endeavor.

"Ashes to ashes. Dust to dust," the preacher intoned in a deep baritone.

As the last rites were given and the remains were placed into the open, awaiting earth, I had a clearer picture of what may have happened years ago in Minters, Alabama. Suddenly, I had a compelling need to see my great-grandfather's gravesite. I wanted to see it and try to get a clearer picture of the man he might have been. Perhaps his headstone could tell me something. I looked through the old rustic cemetery for his name on a headstone, some of which were weathered and eroded by time. I went through most of it thinking I could find it somewhere. When I grew tired of searching, I asked Dad, knowing he could point it out to me.

"Where is your grandfather, Dad? Is he here?"

"Nah, son, he's at a white cemetery a few miles away."

When he said that, I went cold, paused, and looked for a response. There were really no words to explain the vacuum created at the time, but something was sucked right out of me. "Oh really?" or "You don't say?" or even "Sho 'nuff?" were the furthest words from my mind. Why was Dad so nonchalant in answering my question as if I should have known better? I exploded internally.

That bastard, that lousy, white redneck bastard, I thought.

When I saw the "cross-generational watermelon truck," bobbing and weaving and spilling its load in bright, contrasting colors, and ultimately rotting in a grayish-brownish heap, he was the driver. As if that was not enough, he left the scene, accepting no blame. He went back to his own side of town, cleaned up the evidence, closed the garage door, and hoped there were no witnesses.

It was foolish to think I would find him in the black folks' cemetery. He was white—pure white. He was my grandmother's father though, and my grandmother was the real bastard, not him. I guess to him, at the time, it was the only sensible thing to do. Did he ever imagine that his great-grandson of another race would, one day, seek him out of the past for whatever reason? Did he care? What were his motivations? Were they control, lust, manipulation, or all of the above? Did he try to turn back the hands of time? Did he really love my great-grandmother? Something in this picture puzzled and angered me. Was this why seeing a black woman with a white man angered me at times? Why were black women considered safer than the black men in today's work force? What do white men in power really think about black women? How does the corporate structure affect the relationship of black men and women? The cubicle has many faces.

"Come on, son. I want you to meet your white ainty," Dad said.

I froze.

What the fu ... All right, all right! I thought. *Why was he making such a big thing of this "white thing"? Did he think they held greater value because they were white? I don't know these people. Why couldn't she just be my "ainty" or my aunt, for that matter? Why was Dad so gung-ho over something that had no prize? Could he write a check and someday cash in on what he seemed to value so much? What were the benefits of this? Were they even worth mentioning?*

I grew tired and needed to regroup. Although I appeared silent, my mind roared like a Michigan truck plant in full operation. Off to my side, I could see Jim talking with the two white men I first thought were undertakers. They were the old woman's sons, making them my uncles—uncles that I never knew existed until this day. Jim was talking and seemingly having the time of his life with his newly discovered relatives. He could play the game well, at times better than I could.

Since meeting the white folks meant so much to Dad, I went along with it. It wasn't hard. The immediate circumstances only made it that way. Conversely, I think about my experiences at a predominately all-black college, fifteen years prior, where I really didn't feel I fit in. A working, off-campus student that took a long time to adjust to a climate of fierce competition, materialism, and favoritism, I was slow to appreciate the advantages of black college life. Some of my favorite instructors, Dr. Nash and Dr. Meredith, were white. I could always talk to them even when other instructors seemed rushed. They both looked like survivors of the '60s drug, hippie era. We gravitated towards one another probably because, to me, they were approachable, and we were all deviants in a conformist environment. It did not matter that I was black and they were white. What mattered was they were real people who supported me even when the administration occasionally did not. It was an environment of simulated class systems and contradicting moral structures that, at the time, clashed with my perception of reality. If I didn't fit in there with people just like me, I wondered when and where I would.

My transition from a black Southern Baptist college to a Northern white Catholic college run by Jesuit nuns years later took me from one extreme to another. I was finally serious about completing my coursework and contemplated becoming a teacher. The school, Marygrove College, gave me every tool I needed—including money. Dr. Schaeffer, Dr. Rashid, and Dr. Woodard would tear my papers to shreds while, at the same time, telling me that I was a good writer with great potential. They challenged me to improve. Being a product of a black institution, I challenged them as well.

Dr. Schaeffer taught a course called "Faulkner, Hemingway, and Fitzgerald," which required reading eleven books from the three authors. I did not care for Faulkner. I groused that his novels were offensive in their depiction of blacks.

"His message is not worth the effort of reading the novel," I charged.

Although Faulkner was a proponent of his era, he often used black images in a negative light, something I would never do as a writer. I questioned if Faulkner, himself, was a racist, just as I questioned my own views. When we finally went on to the next author, Hemingway, everyone was relieved because the feuding ended. Hemingway was a great writer who wrote about heroism, life's challenges, and successes through simplicity. I was captivated by his work "A Clean, Well-Lighted Place" and struggled to understand why he took his own life so violently. My best essays came from his work because he didn't play the race card, and his work was universal, not a reversal. When I saw Dr. Schaeffer later that year, she told me she was planning to revamp the course—a course she had been teaching for ten years.

Chapter 16

It was time to meet the white people—my relatives. There was no reason to delay any longer because I had spun my wheels long enough, both during this episode and many times in life. The anger that I felt towards my great-grandfather must end with my great-grandfather. I could not charge his family for a tab he walked out on generations ago. It was a losing battle. I was angry though only because I wished at the time that my great-grandfather never walked in the picture generations ago because of the way he disappeared and because of what he may have passed on to my brother. If I continued to be angry about something I could not change, I was only hurting myself, and I knew this. It was now time to grow up and change the world according to how I saw it—one city block or one country mile at a time.

I joined my father about ten feet to my left as he was standing next to the old white woman who I thought appeared more grandeur than she deserved. She was about seventy years old, with grayish-white hair. She was a rather peaceful-looking woman who looked as if she had lived through the struggles of others as well as her own. I would respect her because her age and experiences warranted it, and that was the way I was brought up. Besides, I didn't have anything against her unless she had a problem with me. Why would she? I didn't come for my share of the land, the wealth, or even the mule. I was only there to pay my respects and to answer a few questions. I wanted to know more about the family tree and where I fit in. If I became an effigy in this script, it would be better to know now so I could fight it "tooth and nail." Unlike my father, I did not want to look back blindly over my past with regrets and questions (although I doubt he regrets much). I think too much. I had to know in order to build a fortress from my great-grandfather's misdeeds.

I cast my eyes on the old woman. I looked on at her attentively as she talked to another, unaware of being watched. When she finished, she turned and her icy bluish-gray eyes met brown eyes. I looked away feeling I was staring at her. I knew granddad Allen

Kirk Coleman

Coleman's deep dark brow was capable of intimidation, and this was not what I wanted to do. Besides, it did not take much to see that she and her sons were the only "ones" there, and it probably took all they had to come. They were a minority although the other people there varied from "blue black," as they said, to "light, bright, damned-there white."

I smiled inside with reason. Today, in this place, they were minorities because they were white—pure white, a twist of fate leavened years ago by only one man.

Our next meeting was more congenial and more planned than the first. Our eyes were ready for each other this time. It happened the same time I heard Dad say what he'd been trying to say for a while.

"This is your great-ainty. This is my son, Kirk," he said.

As he spoke, I listened to every word he said, acutely focusing on the old woman while anticipating that adjective that irked me so. This time he did not use that word! He did not use the word that his mother used so frequently to elevate and protect herself from the scores of people she grew up with in the old South. He did not use the word that he, himself, was programmed to draw upon when he needed to rise above the ashes of his own culture. He did not use the word that made me realize that regardless of who I was and regardless of what I became, this was what I was not, and I was okay with that. I was perfectly okay.

I extended my arm to her, and we touched hands for the first time in life.

"How are you, I'm Kirk."

"Hi, Kirk. I have heard so much about y'all. I told your dad to bring you to Huntsville to visit sometime," she said politely in polished Southern dialect.

My father was one of the few remaining relatives on the "dark side" that kept in contact and visited her even before her half-brother, Uncle Willie, passed.

"Okay ... uh ... sure. I'll come with my dad one day soon. It was nice meeting you. Are you going to the family dinner at the house?" I asked.

"No, I'm gonna' stop at my son's house up the road and head back for Huntsville," she said.

"Nice meeting you," I said.

"You, too," she responded politely.

I joined Jim in a conversation with the two white men, her sons, who were said to be my uncles. We talked about vintage cars, laughed, and exchanged numbers until we were the only ones there. We said we would call and, perhaps, one day visit them and welcomed them to come to Detroit as well. Like many people there, I never expected to see them again—the white people. Such experiences happened only once in life and this was a lifetime for me. I got the keys from Jim and brought the car closer to remind him we must leave soon. The real world awaited us.

As we said goodbye and drove towards the log cabin house, I wondered about the experience that took place before me. I wondered if, despite my mind's rage, I was sociable enough towards my white relatives. I wondered if I were in their shoes, would I be afforded the same courtesy. I also wondered why a passerby sped by a suburban Detroit gas station as I was getting gas one night and called me that "N" word in 1998, two years before the turn of the century? I wondered when this race thing would go too far, and if I were the weary child who was tired of playing the game moments before taking the pieces and scattering them about the room. I grew tired of the world telling me I had to "cross-over" to be truly successful. I grew tired of the same man looking over my resume, smiling, and telling me I needed my degree, so I got my degree. When I came back with my degree, there was that same man sitting at the desk telling me something else was needed—something I did not have. I was getting to a point where his approval meant nothing to me.

* * *

We drove about a half mile down the two-way highway and turned right down a secluded red-dirt road. As we drove slowly up the road about eighty yards, the thickly clad pine trees gave way to automobiles, and I could see the log cabin house in the distance. In the background I saw what appalled me as a child—the outhouse—now converted to a storage shed. Modern technology had finally reached the log cabin. To see the late model cars lined up near the log cabin that I had not seen in almost thirty years caused a peculiar clash in my mind's eye. This was a house built almost one hundred years ago, before cars were even invented. We parked and walked to what looked like a family gathering outside the house.

I could see Linda's brothers from Texas, the "twin towers," towering over the crowd, close to seven feet tall. This was their father's home and they came to see him for the last time. We played together on the same soil almost thirty years ago when we were young. DeMal was just a baby. It seemed that my life had, at least, come half circle just being there. Having walked this same soil over sixty years ago, I could only imagine how Dad was feeling.

When Jim and I walked into the crowd of people, we were greeted by some, while others just watched. We did not know everyone there, but everyone knew Dad and knew about us. His mother Jessie and Uncle Willie were brother and sister. Instead of trying to meet new people, we went for people we already knew because no one there seemed outwardly friendly. I found Linda and her sister, gave them both long hugs, and told them they were from Mom.

"'Sup, cuz," Jim said as we greeted the twin towers (although they were not twins). We gave them a hug. As Jim stood next to the tallest one, I noticed how Jim, at six feet two, barely came up to his shoulder. This cousin was towering over Jim. One of the two, "Duck," was nicknamed to help him avoid hitting his head on objects most people missed. They inherited the height from their forefathers in giant

Kirk Coleman

proportion. Even Linda, the youngest daughter, was well over six feet. Her own daughter is six foot three, going to school on a basketball scholarship. I always wondered if they would be all right, free from the condition. There had been some talk about someone of the same stature dying prematurely of heart-related symptoms. This, of course, was a pattern I did not hope to find. This was my family.

The male lion is the most feared animal in the jungle. He dominates his habitat with predator instincts that are awesome. At the top of the food chain, looking down, the male lion can pick and choose the hunt with little fear of being hunted himself. Animals keep their distance, careful not to invade his territory, while others on his menu avoid him completely. He is an over-sized cat on steroids with the terrain capability of a Sherman tank. He kills when he is hungry. He kills when he is angry. He kills ... just for the kill. The lion is tactful and confident in even the simplest function. The lion knows he is a lion. He knows that he was born of a lion—king of the jungle. Men marvel at his spirit and use the lion to fortify what is courageous, true, and just, even when they fall short. The lion has the qualities that we revel and admire most. He is king with God-like attributes.

Whether stalking, walking, or running, he is the ultimate vision of symmetry. Even with blood on his mane and teeth, he licks his paws, yawns, and becomes the cuddly animal on the shelf all over again. He not only writes the manual of jungle law, but also sets the groundwork as well. Nothing is fair. It is, after all, a jungle out there and all that counts is survival—his own. Being king certainly has its rewards. If the lion is what it is without any input from mankind, one can only imagine the force that created him. No scientist or institution can claim him. He is of a force certainly greater than we. When governments collapse, a lion is still a lion. When NASDAQ surges or declines, the lion remains the same. He is of a force we, as humans, simply cannot control.

Despite all, it would be foolish to believe even the lion lives free of struggles. When it suckles its mother, the young lion experiences fierce competition firsthand. The sights and sounds of other animals looming with their own instincts remind the young lion that danger is only yards away. The mother can only protect him for so long. She teaches him to hunt while the male, the father, hunts only for himself. When the young lion matures, he learns that his greatest dangers may come from members of his own species. Mating and territorial disputes among lions cause the fiercest battles of Crusade proportions. Like many animals, it is common for the old and young of the same species to battle in a quest for survival. This is the jungle. Here, hostile takeovers are a way of life—they started here.

* * *

There were tables scattered about the front lawn where people were sitting, eating, and drinking sodas. A large maple tree towered high above the congregation, keeping the hot sun at bay. People came in and out of the house with plates, letting us know where the food was being served. Although we were both hungry, we planned to eat light because our cousins on my mother's side back in Birmingham were taking us out to a seafood buffet later that night.

I was thirsty and looked in a plastic can with ice for something to drink, hoping to find a Mountain Dew. I was flipping and panning through the icy water until my hand almost froze; I settled for a generic grape soda to quench my thirst. I handed one to Jim, and we walked to Dad seated in the shade. Despite the few people I knew, I didn't want to eat until everyone knew who we were. If they saw Dad with us, they would know who we were. They would know we were his sons, relatives from Detroit.

"Hey, Dad."

"Hey, my sons. You guys hungry? Go in the house and get you something."

Little did Dad know this was the invitation I was waiting for. I walked off and left Jim and Dad at the table. Up the stairs of the log cabin house, I went in search of Southern cuisine. In the living room to the right was the buffet table with aluminum pots and pans that, as a caterer, I dared not review. It was a simple affair with no skirts, cloths, floral arrangement, or elevation. There were no petite pastries of exotic origin. There were no scents of herbs and spices from a faraway land. There were no chef jackets or tuxedoed waiters anywhere in sight. There was only a simple old lady serving, the same that did most of the cooking. The menu: fried chicken, barbecued ribs, and smoked neck bones, with turnip greens, candied yams, and cornbread. I approached the table.

"How ya doin'?" I said in intentionally-broken English.

"All right. What you like?"

"It looks real good. I'd like a little bit of everything."

"Okay, what piece of chicken you like?"

"White meat—a breast," I answered.

"We ain't got no breasts!" she snapped. "All we have is legs, wings, and thighs. No white meat heah," she said dryly.

"Okay, give me a leg," I said, trying to end the conversation quickly.

I wondered if I said the wrong thing and came off as the condescending Northerner with extravagant tastes, but I only asked for a breast.

"You wont cake?" she said, almost mechanically, clashing with my view of hospitality.

"Yeah ... uh—please."

When she lowered the pound cake in my plate, I said thanks, tried to smile, and left immediately. When I walked out Jim was walking up to the porch for a plate as well.

"Looks good," he said.

"Yeah, it does. Go and get a plate, but before you do let me tell you something," I said, pulling him closer to whispering length.

"What is it?" he asked.

"When you go up to the food table, don't ask for white meat."

"What?"

"The lady at the food table blasted me for asking for white meat like I was from another planet, man."

He looked confused.

"Just don't ask for white meat," I said.

He went in the house grinning, shaking his head.

I sat down next to Dad, who was seated with Uncle Mack and Willie C., my Grandfather Allen Coleman's brother and nephew, who came to pay their respects. I could tell there was dissension somewhere in this picture with these people I called my relatives. I could detect coldness from those I didn't know. I sought explanations to understand in my mind. Where were the white folks and why didn't they come to the family dinner? Was there bad blood between the black and white factions that made up this family? Did we crash-land in the middle of this ordeal by being friendly to the whites? Why was the "white meat" thing blown out of proportion? I was curious.

"Dad, is there any reason that some of the people here don't like the others?"

"What do you mean—uh, they get along okay. I don't know if liking each other has anything ...."

"Let me put it this way. Why are none of the white people here now?" I asked.

"My ainty came from Huntsville and is visiting her son before she goes back tonight, like she said.

Besides, all mothers want to see their children sometimes."

"Yeah. This ainty is your grandfather's ...."

"She is my grandfather's daughter by a white mother," he said.

"Is she wealthy?" I asked.

"Oh, yeah, when I was tight she sent me three hundred dollars so quick, it made my head spin," he laughed.

"Who inherited your grandfather's land and wealth?" I asked.

"The lady and her two sons."

"The white ones," I added.

Getting tired of questions, Dad asked, "So where are you going with this?"

"I don't know. What I do know is the tension is thick around here and the friendliest people we met here today may have been white," I said.

"Sometimes white folks can be just as nice as anybody else. I've met some friendly white folks in my life," he said.

"So have I. Sometimes I just question their motives."

Jim was coming out of the log cabin house as I was examining its architecture and design. I cast my eyes on the old house with the thought that I may never see it again. *Such a rich history behind it*, I thought. Perhaps one day I would have a house built like this, with modern-day amenities, of course, for my great-grandchildren, five generations. Wood is a gift of nature. Nothing is so natural, durable, and almost eternal at the same time.

As if it was yesterday, I could picture DeMal outside the house, tall, lanky, out of his stroller, running freely with red dirt on his high-top orthopedic leather shoes. He would run after the football as we threw it to the older boys. He would hold it and delay our game and we, as kids, would rush him to give the ball up. If given the chance, in contrast to the original picture, I would pick him up, hug him, and make him the quarterback.

Jim sat down at the table, and we ate and talked about our experiences.

"Did you have any problems at the buffet table?" I asked.

"No. She wasn't too friendly, but I just wanted a wing anyway."

"Good. She has the personality of a vending machine, but can you detect that some of the people here are acting strange?"

"Yeah."

"Not the ones we know, the ones we really don't know," I explained.

"Well, I didn't come to make friends, just to pay my respects," Jim said.

"You know, I think the white relatives had something to do with it. We spent a lot of time with them. Some of the people here probably have mixed feelings toward them."

"You think so?"

"It must be something. Why didn't the white folks come by the house after the funeral?"

"I don't know. Ready to leave?" he asked.

"Yeah, let's go."

"Dad's not goin' back to Birmingham until later, but Uncle Mack is going now, so we could follow him back," Jim said.

"Cool. Now we don't have to worry about getting lost again."

"I know the way back," Jim replied.

"Yeah, right," I added sarcastically. "Let's follow Mack anyway."

We said goodbye to Dad who mentioned he would call us in Birmingham in the morning to meet for coffee. We said goodbye to those we knew and offered condolences for the last time. But to some we left anonymously, with no word at all, knowing whatever rift was created could not be fixed at this time.

Jim took the wheel; I didn't expect to drive for the short distance back. We pulled out, following the late model Cadillac up the two-lane winding roads, only stopping for gas and Mountain Dews at a little station. Our mission was almost complete. I thought about my experiences and attempted to put them in perspective until regrettably, I fell asleep before we reached the historic bridge of Selma. I wanted to see it in modern-day form, at the same time imagine what it must have been like with the police, the attack dogs, the fire hoses, and the utter chaos occurring. I wonder if any of the people we just left were there.

Chapter 17

When I woke up, the car was stopping in front of Sook's house. I didn't know if Jim woke me or the change in movement did. My watch said 6:30 p.m., so I knew immediately it was 5:30 in Birmingham. The sun was setting, the heat was ceasing, and it was rather pleasant outside. When we got out and walked to the house, the wooden door was ajar. We knocked on the screen door. Linda came to the door to welcome us.

"Hey, you gaz. So hah was the trip?" Linda asked.

"It was nice, but where we went made Birmingham look like New York," Jim said.

"Yeah. I'm glad I took the trip, thanks to Jim," I added.

"Did y'all make it in tahm?"

Jim and I looked at each other with a look that came only from shared personal experiences. We paused, both waiting for the other to respond as if, perhaps, we really didn't know the answer.

"Yeah, we made it in time," Jim said.

"At the right time," I added.

"Well, the phone's been ranging awf the hook 'bout tonight," Linda said.

"So, what do you all have planned?" I asked.

"We're takin' y'all to an awl you kin eat seafood place in I'hn City," she replied.

I knew she meant "Iron City."

As I showered and put on something more comfortable, the telephone rang. It was my second cousin Kat and her husband Vince. They were the planners of the outing that night. They told Linda that after dinner we would meet at their house for the remainder of the night. Whatever they had planned was fine with me. This was family, and they came no closer than this.

It seemed that my first cousins on Dad's side did not even exist. When I was young, every time Dad and his sisters met, there was a fight, and grandma was right in the middle of it. Granddad was the peacemaker. I do not remember much, but I do remember grandma once telling Dad, "I should have flushed you down the toilet." When we were bad as kids, she would say, "Jimmy and Kirk, y'all so mannish. Y'all so mannish, you stink!" When she was really mad, she would tell us we would "bust hell wide open," which, as a kid, gave me profound images of hell exploding if I got there. Nonetheless, when her children met, they would jockey for her favor, with the result usually being chaos. When her children's children, like Jim and me, grew up, we decided that if grandma was no longer here, why even bother to keep in touch with my cousins.

The seafood restaurant had the theme of an old ship with dark wood, anchors, and portholes. In the restaurant, crab cakes, crustaceans, fresh fish, and Coronas seemed to come from all directions. On the table, it would all disappear only to reappear when the swinging kitchen doors swung open. As I looked at the party of twelve, I noticed then that nothing brought people together better than good food. Good food nourishes the mind, body, and spirit, while dinner table discussions are the pathway to family knowledge. It is a ritual of the past that is waning in the micro-techno-pizza-popper world we live in today. People can learn from dinner table discussions if they only listen.

Sitting down and communing as a family is needed today more than ever. Perhaps this was why my mother always told me to *sit down and eat!* It is a ritual started, possibly, in the South, a ritual that the savvy enjoy in four-star capacity, and a ritual that I chose to be a part of many times in my pursuits. I remember preparing tableside items like Bananas Foster, igniting the brandy and watching the flames reach towards the ceiling as caramelized ginger, cinnamon, and brown sugar vapors filled the air. At the same time, the guests' eyes would light up and excitement permeated the room. This is what I loved, lived for, and contemplated leaving, knowing one day I must.

Like a Shakespearean-trained actor who was gifted and loved the art, but who only landed mediocre roles as the "disposable Negro in black exploitation flicks," it was time to consider other options and move on. I could be successful with my own catering business. I have been. Somehow, the way the cards fell, I lost DeMal at the peak of my success; therefore, success really didn't matter in this arena anymore. Did I want to continue at such a fast pace securing and maintaining contracts while love, stability, and the world seemed to pass me by? No. I wanted to marry one day (soon) and was growing tired of the late-night lifestyle that catering parties warranted.

Wine, women, and song were a tempting subculture of gourmet restaurants and the catering business that I wouldn't wish on any married man. There was a majority female clientele who called after business hours, which provided too many opportunities to slip into the night. Someone said women love a man that can cook in and out of the kitchen. There is some validity to that statement. But after a while, anything gets old.

Kirk Coleman

Chyna, a product of an 8-to-5 corporate job, did not like clients calling me throughout the night, which provided me an alibi every time I went out. She was getting restless. I didn't want to lose her by spinning my wheels again. She wanted me to find a Jay-O-Bee now and be an entrepreneur later, if the situation presented itself. This time, grudgingly, I thought she might have been right.

I will never forget the experience of having dinner with my relatives that night. We were having such a good time talking that when DeMal's name came up, there were only smiles and laughter. Like me, he was a son of the North and the South whose life's decisions made the headlines to all that knew him. He was the baby, the youngest of his generation, and the youngest of the first cousins that mattered.

When he was a baby, we watched him like a hawk.

When he was six, we taught him to fight by showing him how to make a fist, swing first, and punch his opponent directly in the face, ultimately making him a knockout artist.

When he was ten, Jim and I counseled him not to make the mistakes we made growing up and reinforced the values Mom often taught us by force. It was not easy though. He never let us forget that we were not his father.

When he was sixteen, he stayed with me for weeks in Atlanta over the summer; I spoiled him. While there, I took him to different colleges and tried to convince him to go to Georgia Tech on a basketball scholarship. He was already six feet (with a size sixteen shoe) and scoring 8 to 14 points a game as a tenth grader. Mom was struggling to keep shoes on his feet because he grew so fast and had to shop where real basketball players shopped.

At seventeen, he knocked a white boy out cold for calling him the "N" word on a hotel elevator where he attended a weekend seminar for student achievement. He also broke his thumb. I told him to watch his temper and swing away from his thumb.

"Use your knuckles," I said.

When he joined the U.S. Air Force at nineteen, we knew he had come of age, old enough to make his own decisions and see the world on his own. He was made for that uniform, a tall, lean, curly-haired, and handsome young man that looked down on the masses and was proud of his stature. He was so handsome even his own cousins fell in love with him—the female ones.

He was stationed on an air base in Germany as a Military Policeman trained in highly destructive weaponry. In his leisure, he and his friends rode their motorcycles all over on the Autobahn, throughout Europe, and as far as the coast of France. My little brother was living a life I could only dream about, even flying in the cockpit of an F-16. I was so proud of him.

In 1990, Iraq invaded Kuwait, and the Persian Gulf War started. We were concerned, but we knew

Kirk Coleman

he was in Germany at the time. U.S. Forces were mobilizing in the area. Threats were made from the podium and slung across the globe via CNN. It all happened so fast. A war was starting, and the most protected member of the tribe was an enlisted warrior. We were restless. I was nervous. Then one night, we got the call.

"This is the international operator. You have a call from Germany. Do you accept the charges?"

Mom answered with anticipation, "Yes, I accept."

"Hey, Mom."

"Hi, son. How are you?"

"I'm fine. Things are somewhat frantic here. I'm getting moved to Saudi Arabia, to an air base there."

"Oh, son, be careful. This is not your war," she said.

"I'll be all right, Mom. Don't worry. My job is to guard the airfield miles away from the action. I'll be okay," he said.

"When do you leave, son?" she asked.

"In the morning, as soon as I take some shots to protect me from chemical warfare. They say Saddam may try to use anthrax, a poisonous gas."

"So what is it you're taking?" she asked.

"I don't know, but someone said it's probably a strain of the same stuff Saddam has. Everyone has to take it. We don't have a choice, and you know how I feel about needles."

"Son, my prayer is that God watch over you and keep you safe, and I know He will."

"I'll be fine, Mom. Don't worry. I gotta go," he said.

"I love you, son. Take care."

"I love you too, Mom."

She was right, as far as I was concerned. This really wasn't his war. His war was oblivious to the white soldiers who fought by his side. His war was in a different arena. It took place on American soil, in the financial institutions, universities, insurance agencies, and employment lines thereof. It didn't involve an enemy that could be identified, pinpointed, and extracted easily. His war followed him to sleep at night and woke him in the morning. How did I know so much about his war? It was my own, and I am convinced that some will forever remain oblivious to it.

The Persian Gulf War involved power, resources, and world dominance. This same system welcomed and drafted my forefathers to fight its enemies, only later to embrace that same enemy over my forefathers' sweat, blood, and tears. This was my brother and, although I've seen it many times before, he was too valuable a sacrifice for a freedom, liberty, and justice that paid me little mind. History taught me this.

During World War II my grandfather fought in the navy for the freedom of this great country, as well as his own. He was drafted. He was a security policeman who spent most of his tour controlling the Filipino shores on a PT boat like John F. Kennedy. When he came home to Alabama in the '40s, Jim Crow laws permeated the liberties he fought so hard to defend, while incarcerated Japanese Americans were compensated for their detainment. Unlike John F. Kennedy who went on to become President, my grandfather, Allen Coleman, became a janitor at a state university, and a very good one.

My father was on the front lines of the Korean War in the early '50s. As he rode on a train full of American troops, a sniper shot him and missed his heart by less than two inches. He almost died that day. He was relocated to a base in Texas to recover from his wound and granted a leave to see his family in Alabama. He would receive the Purple Heart for being wounded in action when he returned to duty. While he was in Alabama, he met my mother Ludeal Lampkin, who was a classmate of his sister Lubertha, at Miles College.

My father was a handsome man in his heyday, but my mother was both pretty and smart. Having traveled around the world with many different women at many different ports (and having abandoned children in Germany, the Philippines, and Texas), he fell in love with her and asked her to wait for him to finish his tour in Germany. When he returned he would ask for her hand in marriage. The two were young and in love and the world offered many rich possibilities ... at that time.

When he arrived in Germany, he faced some of the same hostilities he had come to know in the United States in the South. Three off-duty military policemen confronted him one night at a bar and told him to leave. When he questioned why, the answer,

"No niggers allowed. This is a white bar only—soldier boy!" incensed him so. As he turned around and left to avoid confrontation, the fear he experienced turned to anger.

Did I risk my life for this shit? he thought.

He went back to his barracks and told two buddies, Ron Dash and Paul Brown, what happened. They had a plan. The three men sneaked through a hole in a back fence because they had no passes, hoping to find the three soldiers. When they walked in the bar, they found the three drunken soldiers and settled the score. My father declared war on the three men—his own war. The drunken soldiers never knew what hit them. Bottles were broken on heads, noses and arms were broken, and a medic was alerted. The bar was in shambles. As the three men slipped back through the fence, they went to their barracks as if nothing happened, but they knew there was more to it than that. Later that night my dad and his friends were arrested and faced a court martial for "Inciting a Riot" and "Assault."

Ron Dash was scheduled to finish his tour in the next two days, then go home, so Dad lied and said Ron was not there. A senior officer on tour with Dad in Korea, a white man, got Dad out of it. He, to this day, has not received his Purple Heart, even after numerous formal requests. If he never gets it, I am still proud of what he did that night in Germany. Although times have changed, almost fifty years later, I guess I am like him in many ways.

Chapter 18

The dinner party was winding down. Everyone seemed to have their fill of crustaceans, Coronas, and conversation, as well as pitchers of Mountain Dew. As I looked around the table of twelve, each face meant something different to me. Each face had its own distinct history of joy, sadness, profound grief, and struggle in my mind's eye. Each face had its own story to tell, as many do, when they reach a certain point in life. I thought of the Last Communion with Jesus and His twelve disciples, where they ate bread and drank wine while discussing information that would affect humanity for years to come.

We just talked and passed family information. To me, there were stories behind each face, whether wrinkling and graying or new to life. Some stories were greater and some lesser than the others. Some had tragic endings, and some had joyous beginnings. In each story there was a lesson learned, whether it was kept private or passed to another.

Looking at my cousin Johnny, who lost his son, Jonathan, to senseless violence when Jonathan had returned from the navy, I could still see the loss in his eyes. At the same time, his eyes would light up when Asia, his granddaughter, was mentioned. Knowing this, whenever I saw him, I only talked about Asia. This was probably why everyone spent so much time talking about baby DeMal, and I thanked them for doing so. DeMal and Jonathan, second cousins, both passed when their children were very young.

We moved our gathering to Kat and Vince's home to let our food digest and to relax. There we listened to Joy and Faith, their twins, sing old Baptist hymns while Vince played the guitar. The men then left and went out to the adjacent garage where most men go to relax. Leaving the women and kids in the house, we had time to spend the last part of our journey with Raymond, Johnny, and Eugene, the first cousins who were like brothers to us, although at a distance. Vince was there too. It was he that hosted this gathering at his home, and he was a welcome addition to the family through marriage. He treated my cousin and the twins like queens. Working a

Kirk Coleman

second job part-time at a pawnshop, he had many toys to keep us occupied.

"Y'all wanna see my guns?" he asked.

"Yeah," Jim responded.

He went to the closet and unloaded what appeared to be an arsenal on the ironing board.

"What do you have?" I asked.

"Ah got an AK 47, a Tek 9, a Street Sweepa, a 30 R6, a M16, and some pistols," he replied.

"Man ... why so many weapons? You could have won the civil war from your garage," I added.

"When ah see somethin' that gets pawned, ah put it aside and get it if I wont it. I jus' collect 'em and would only use 'em to protect mah family," he said.

I did a quick analysis of my second cousin. Vince sang and played in the church choir. He was a good and understanding father to his kids. He was a good son to his own mother. He was a good son-in-law to his wife's mother, Linda. He was a loving husband to his wife, Kat. He worked hard and earned an honest living. He was a typical example of what God can do with one who listened. He had fears though, of his own people and of others, with good reason. I hoped he kept his fears in perspective and kept his museum of destruction in its cases. If he continued collecting guns and never used them, there's no telling how many lives might be saved because everyone is not like Vince.

It was midnight as Vince pulled a beautiful base guitar out of its case. It sparkled with a gold-cream color and looked exotic and expensive. He said it came from a bass player of a famous band who pawned it for money. Vince pulled out his amplifier and plugged it up to the guitar, then started playing and singing. I carefully put the AK 47 down and went over to look and listen. After singing about four tunes, he paused. Jim asked for the guitar. The three Coronas must have given him courage. Jim played with it for a while, but I really didn't expect much. I knew Jim had a guitar once, a beautiful, spearmint-green one. Dad had brought it home. It was humorous, yet sobering at the same time, to watch Jim, an intelligent man, play the guitar like an eight year old. It was almost as if he never had had a guitar, the way he played. As mysteriously as his guitar appeared, it disappeared, never to return.

After a few more laughs, we decided to wrap things up and started the process of saying goodbye. We had to go back to Sook's (or Linda's house) to get some sleep before we left Sunday morning for Detroit. My watch said 1:15 a.m. I still could not believe the ground we covered in such little time. Now we were soon to be headed back for the last seven hundred fifty miles.

Back at the house, I packed my weekend supply of clothes in order to leave early in the morning. Jim did the same. I called Chyna to check in and fell asleep immediately afterwards, as if I had a full day's work behind me. Jim called his wife. After a good night's sleep, we left Sunday morning at 7:45 with only Linda seeing us off, waving from the porch I knew so well. We stopped at a large station just off Highway 65 to say goodbye to Dad, get some gas, and a morning coffee. Dad was staying a few more days with some relatives in Birmingham. He was retired and didn't have to rush as we did. I found cappuccinos instead of regular coffee and bought one for each of us.

In parting, I remembered a jazz-inspirational tape I had loaned Dad, <u>The Brand New Heavies</u>, so I asked for it. He reluctantly looked in the glove compartment and returned it. I knew he wanted to keep it longer, but I wanted to hear my favorite song, "Sometimes you gotta do right to be happy." I stuck it in the player as we said goodbye and left, headed back North. This was the last time our feet were on Alabama soil for a while.

Chapter 19

It must have been weeks since I'd seen or talked to my brother Jim. His job and family kept him busy; my pursuits did the same. I made the training for the cellular phone company and was authorized to sell their products. It was May and things blossomed. It was time to get back to work with my bush sculpture and pond business with about forty repeat clients, as well as new referrals. I could always count on catering to bring business in the spring and summer for weddings, family reunions, and company picnics. At the time, I was doing a weekly Jamaican stir-fry at a popular club called Club Network and still had the

Harmonie Park area locked down for catering. I had total autonomy, which I desired, but something was wearing on me. I didn't have the capital or structure to sit back and watch my business run. I was the heart of my business. I was my business. I was becoming a slave to my own choices in life with no one to blame. It seemed inevitable one way or another.

In a move that major corporations use to access long-term growth or loss in business and make changes accordingly, I evaluated my business according to a simple procedure using time versus profit. It seemed my life needed the same.

Recently, selling seven cellular phones with only a page of paperwork netting six hundred forty dollars, I decided that cellular phones were in high demand and would be easy. That amount of money was not bad for a day's work. The only problem was consistency, and that was a problem. I needed consistency. A long-term analysis, however, concluded that one day, the market would be saturated with these phones. I would ride it out while it was good and abandon it later.

Landscaping design was therapeutic and a means to stay in shape. The smell of fresh-cut pines aroused my senses, and the rays of the sun invigorated me. However, the bigger the job, the more labor it required. I sometimes had to pay each of my help up to one hundred twenty-five dollars a day to move up to three tons of stone, if the job warranted it. Since the work was seasonal, I had time to regroup and wouldn't burn myself out, but it was extremely hard work. I had to choose which jobs I would take while servicing repeat clientele. I didn't want to get into anything over my head.

Catering was perhaps the hardest of my gifts to restructure. I trained for this in Atlanta. When I returned and did the Gil Hill for the city council party in 1989, my catering career took off. To mansions in the posh Indian Village of Detroit, I was there. To radio promotions for recording artists—including Aaliyah, I was there. To elegant atrium events sponsored by a corporate sponsor, I was there. To the old museum of African-American History while the new Charles Wright Museum was under construction, I was there. I wondered, in catering, was there anything left to do?

Catering was extremely time-consuming and relied on preparation and intense time constraints. Selling parties was the initial phase that takes hours determining the clients' needs over the phone and in person. Shopping parties was the next phase. A caterer could spend hours at the market looking for the best buys and highest quality products. Finally, cooking, set up, and delivery were equally important, as well as menu-sensitive variables that only experience dictated.

As far as profit is concerned, catering paid well if the delicate balance of costs and labor was maintained. When a caterer achieved notoriety in the profession, he or she could charge from ten dollars to twenty-five dollars per person only after a track record of accomplishment. When you are new and you compete with established caterers, you best keep your prices low if you want any play. I didn't do anything for under ten dollars per person with a few exceptions (charity work). Also, male caterers beware: A beautiful woman with a "limited budget" could walk in at any time. This I know firsthand. Catering is a luxury. Make her pay your price, plus gratuity.

    Lastly, I looked at the future down the road a few years. I didn't see myself still in this profession as I am today. My mentor Leonardo Fostino, "Lenny," died in his mid-forties of a heart attack at the height of his career. Even chef Lenn, my partner at the museum, has been in the hospital four times that I know of in the last year. I know about the stress that comes with catering firsthand. An era in my life was ending, and I had nothing else to prove. When eras ended, it was time to move on.

    The '70s were an era that some like me found hardest to forget. As a young man, I was in the developmental stages of my life when the '70s were thrust upon me. As a child in the back seat at the drive-in watching "Shaft in Africa," "Superfly," and "The Mack," I began to assimilate what was in fashion from what I saw on the screen. Added to that pressure, some of my schoolmates came to school in the latest fashions. Styles were changing; even the simplest shirt came with wider collars. Elevator shoes, stacks, and bump toes were the latest craze, with higher being cooler. We would compete for the biggest Afro, and the biggest 'fro always seemed to get the prettiest girl. Windowpane jeans were in, and the words "get down" were not demeaning language used to keep one in place.

Kirk Coleman

The early '70s were an era of unity and identity, where the black fist on the pick symbolized a movement, a struggle, and a common link shared by a common people. Of course there were pimps, hustlers, and the infamous pushermen, but the men in the dashikis and large Afros always seemed to prevail and bring order. Even "Superfly" had a dream, a plan for a better life, as many did in this era. An undercurrent of militancy marked this era as one to bring about social change from a people who would not tolerate reliving the '60s. I was born in the '60s but, to me, that era was diluted, vague, and fast, like a Charlie Chaplain movie. The '70s were what I remember most.

When eras ended, there was no newscast or headline to announce that a way of life was coming to a close. Eras didn't end on a certain day or year, conveniently welcoming the next. It was only when form and function no longer benefited the mores of individuals or society that an era must end. When it was over, it was undeniably over. No one had to tell me when the fashion era of the '70s ended. I remember, too well, the last day I wore platform shoes.

That November, the winter of '75, a blanket of snow covered the ground. I had got DeMal dressed and out to elementary school. Now it was time to get ready myself. I was a seventh grader, attending the middle school only three blocks up the street. Jim left an hour earlier to attend high school miles away. Mom was at work. Dad wasn't home. I rushed to get my clothes together, regretting not doing it the night before. I looked in the drier for my gym shoes, and they were wet.

I had ten minutes to make it to school.

I looked in the closet and pulled out the black and white four-inch platforms Dad bought me for Easter, strapped them on my feet, grabbed my books, and rushed out.

I had eight minutes before the bell would ring.

When I stepped outside, I noticed that it had rained the night before and froze, covering the snow that had already fallen. With my eyes on the ground watching each step I took, I carefully walked up the street to avoid slipping. Finally, clearing my block, I looked up at the unpaved snow and ice-covered dirt road and contemplated my journey ahead. I proceeded with caution.

I had five minutes before the bell would ring.

I took a few steps. The snow would not give an inch. I slipped and fell into the ice-packed snow. I got up and continued, wondering if I should go on. I took a few more steps, slipped, lost my balance, avoided falling, but hurt my ankle. In my mind, I heard my grandfather say humorously, "They made platform shoes so black folks can't run from the police." This time I didn't laugh. I wanted to sit in the snow and regroup with my head in my hands, but I could not. I was in middle school now.

I needed a plan for I feared falling again at such high altitudes. Then I saw the fence that ran alongside the road, separating it from the field we called the Army Camp. I held onto the fence, making my way to school praying, "Lord, if I could just make it to school,

I will never, ever, ever wear platforms again." When I got there, I felt so out of place. I could not wait for the day to end so I could take those shoes off and never be seen in them again. No one had to tell me that era was over. I knew firsthand.

It must have been months since the trip we took to Minters, Alabama. I felt like I came up short of really knowing what happened there. I felt that the information I was getting from Dad was subjective, because he admired his white grandfather as I did my own, and I could not blame him for that. I needed someone different, someone old, wise, and impartial to take me to Minters one last time. Like a fly on the wall, an outsider, I needed the objectivity of a camera's eyes to tell me what really happened.

I looked up and down the family tree for one who lived in Minters and still lives today. Sadly, there were not many to fit my criteria, but after some research, my Aunt Unis came to mind. She was my grandfather Allen Coleman's younger sister. She was not a Small. Most importantly, she had no reason to tell me anything but the truth. This is what I gathered from her, as well as the previously compiled information necessary to tell this story—perhaps the most significant one of all.

In the mid- to late-1800s in the South, it was a time of buying and selling human beings, which provided a path to success and prosperity. It was said that the South was made of these classes: planters (plantation and slave owners), yeoman farmers (aspiring landowners, skilled workers), landless whites, and finally free blacks, mulattos (mixed), and slaves. Like a corporation, the class system did not allow much room for mobility, especially at the lower levels.

The American dream existed then, as it does now. Today, a good job with security, a home with brass doorplates, a Volvo station wagon, complete with kids, good schools, and a dog is chic. The white picket fence, a relic of the past, is gone now, replaced with the trendier electronic fence.

In the mid- to late-1800's, the American dream in the South was different because it promoted success at the expense of free human labor, systematically making its laborers feel unworthy of anything but room and board while profits were made. Most landless whites aspired to own land and slaves, while yeoman farmers aspired to be like planters.

On the other end of the spectrum, free blacks, mulattos, and slaves struggled to survive capitalism at its very worst. This, at one time, was the American dream—an exclusionary vision that, to this day, makes even the most outspoken white cringe with disbelief, denial, and dismissal. Where do we go from here?

Moving up a few years, shortly after the Dred Scott Decision, the Kansas-Nebraska Act, and the Civil War which cost 2.8 billion dollars and a million lives, America was under Reconstruction. The war was over, and human slave labor was abolished, but not immediately as some would think. The planters, investors of the war, mislead slaves to think that they were not free; they often resorted to violent, rough tactics to keep them under submission, such as family separation and division. By law, the business of slavery had no form or function in the American landscape, although some held true to its ideals for a very long time.

In the spirit of Willie Lynch, Jim Crow laws took over where American law left off, creating a scourge of violence and lawlessness which sought to resist change. To many blacks, it was safer being back at the plantation. Of course it would be. At that time, their teaching was limited to agriculture and religion, where they met in small groups only, and they serviced the needs of whites.

It was around 1870 when Willie Small was born in the midst of Reconstruction. What is known is he came from a background of planters in the Dallas and Loundes counties in Alabama, including Minters. Whether he originated from wealthy planters or yeoman farmers is unknown. He did inherit approximately twenty square miles of fertile land that he worked as a child and sold its produce at the market, which the family owned as well. He soon took over the land, knowing the strengths and weaknesses of each plot, and cultivated tobacco, cotton, maple, sugarcane, numerous fruit and vegetables, as well as two hundred head of livestock. At the time, there were still freed slaves who lived on the land, worked it, and never left.

It must have started sometime here when my great-grandmother, Mattie Basket, entered the picture.

Folklore tells me that when Will Small knew he felt something more for her, he gave her a gift of two cows to milk, possibly foreseeing children in the future. More gifts came as the white landowner wooed the young black woman. After the sun went down, he would return to her and stay deep into the night. He loved her. She feared him. He owned her. She could not resist him. On and on it went into the secrecy of the night, a white man and his black mistress in the ultimate submission.

    Shortly after the turn of the century, around 1910, Jessie, Monroe, and Willie Small were born to Mattie Basket and William Small the landowner. The boys were raised to work the rich fertile land at a young age, while Jessie Small cooked, cleaned, and milked cows, which had grown to twenty head. William Small Sr. was about forty years old and taught the boys how to cultivate the land. He favored the boys, but two were not enough. The boys mirrored him in his Abraham Lincoln-like stature and, considering the dark complexion of his mistress Mattie Basket, they still could almost pass for white.

    Unknown to his mistress, Willie Small had a plan. It was under construction miles away, but somewhere on the twenty-mile stretch of land. He had two or three other mistresses and five other children after his first three. When Mattie found out, she threatened to leave the land and go to Birmingham. Like an old horse, he didn't mind if she left.

    "You and Jessie can leave if you wonna. My bawys are stayin' heah wit' me," he said.

Realizing there was little she could do about it, she accepted the seeds of the father that were not her own.

In 1935 Jessie Small was married to Allen Coleman, a local boy from Dallas County. One hot, sunny day, some angry white men with guns were pursuing him over a stolen, or borrowed, mule and came by the house on horses. Jessie was shaken by ten loud, angry knocks at the door and went to see who it was. She went out to talk with them while her small son James Coleman Sr. looked out the door. The men were out for revenge with hate in their eyes.

"We heah for Allen Coleman."

"Tell eem ta brang his black ass out cheah—rat nah!" another man said.

"Sir ... Mista, whatchu' wont wit my husband? He not heah, suh—what he do?" Grandma Jessie asked frantically.

"You sho he ain't in? If I come back, I'll find out myself. Won't be so nas eitha."

"No, suh, I sweah he not heah," she said, looking innocent.

"Tell eem we came to strang his black ass up," the other man said.

"Fo' what ... fo' what? Why you wonna hut mah husban'? Why, suh?" she asked.

"That nigga stole mah mule and damn dar killed' em," he said. "He stole' em and he rode' em till he could barely stand on is own. Nigga almost killed my mule and I'z gonna kill the black son-bitch!"

The men on horses then rode off. The little boy, only three, held on to his mother and wondered what was wrong. He wondered why the white men were so angry and knew then to give them their distance. This day, at a young age, he experienced the fear of the South—a fear that shaped him for life.

It's a good thing granddad wasn't in because he could have lost his life for something he didn't do. The true culprit was "Nigga Oliver," a mischievous, fun-loving prankster known only by that name. He lived on the edge and always seemed to narrowly escape lynching. He stole the old mule and rode it until it could take no more, leaving the mule nearly incapacitated in the field. It was all fun and innocent role-playing. Perhaps Nigga Oliver was trying to collect on a debt. Whatever the case, the implications were endless. He told someone that my grandfather stole and rode the mule, and the word spread.

The men were not quick to take action because they could tell Jessie Coleman was a first generation mulatto, which had privileges over being darker at the time. The men knew they might have to answer to another white landowner and possibly a relative for their actions. When William Small found out about the angry men on horses, he took care of the matter immediately. They never returned. Granddad was under the security blanket of William Small as well. William wanted Granddad, his son-in-law, to stay and work the land, but Granddad refused. He wanted to support his family and felt it was better that he left Minters to do so.

Kirk Coleman

In addition to the three mistresses and eight first-generation mulatto children, overseeing numerous sharecroppers, tending to crop production, and stocking and running a store, William Small Sr. had another project in the works just miles away.

In 1945 he was nearing sixty years old and was probably thinking about settling down. He didn't yield enough boys as Monroe and Willie were the only males out of eight children. He married a white woman and had seven more children, four boys and three girls. One of the boys was even named Willie, giving him two sons with the same name—one black and one white. The children, all fifteen of them, grew up on the land as half-brothers and sisters, knowing there were differences. The old man favored his white family and lived with them, while his visits elsewhere were shorter and shorter. Tensions were high as the mistresses discovered what was happening. Even the children could see the changes. The white children had more responsibilities and the mulatto children had more hard work. Of the mixed children, Willie Jr. and Monroe were favored the most. William Sr. never cared too much for girls; they and their mothers were welcome to leave at any time. His new wife didn't care for any of the mistresses and told him to stay away from them. Then one day it all came to a head.

It was said by my Aunt Unis that one day the old man had a work crew cutting the grass on Mattie Basket's plot of land. When Willie Small's wife found out about this, she told him that he must choose between his wife and his mistress. Then she told him to go to Mattie's house and take out everything of value.

"Those black folks are living like white folks," she said.

He hesitated for he knew his sons would take offense, but the woman left him no choice. He went to the house and argued with my great-grandmother as he took the silver, fine linen, and other items of value from of the house. Those items merely sat in a box for years and rotted in a closet at his country store. Soon after the incident, Mattie Basket sadly left for Selma. The family that never really was faded back ... back ... back into the annals of history's past.

Fact, fiction, and folklore—this is what was gathered from personal accounts, interviews, and being there myself. I was satisfied with my endeavors after finally learning the truth. Many of my questions were answered about Minters, as well as about some of the occurrences before that time, be they good or bad—but not all. As knowledge does, it only brings more questions since the glass can appear half empty although it is half full. Wisdom is the divine catalyst that says enough is enough or, conversely, demands a further quest for knowledge.

Chapter 20

Lately, there has been a barrage in the media describing the latest breakthroughs in genetic research. These breakthroughs are said to parallel the experience of walking on the moon in the '60s. DNA, chromosomes, gene maps, proteins, and other scientific terminology are now commonplace among ordinary citizens and scientists alike. Genetic law, unheard of twenty years ago, is now the hot topic of debate for fear some will experience the negative effects of the genetic revolution or get left behind.

At its best, genetic research can give answers to dominant or recessive traits, trace human evolution and behavior, and ultimately find a cure for cancer, AIDS, Alzheimer's, and so forth. Researchers claim that the human species is 99.9 percent identical, with people of different races actually closer, genetically, than some individuals of the same race, discounting theories of a superior race

These complex microscopic materials determine how we grow, think, live, and, possibly, how we may die, ultimately linking us to life in a prior existence, whether it is father to son or generations past. Science is taking it a step further, with talk of cloning humans, while private industry dabbles with the idea of selling sperm and eggs on the Internet. This has spurned debates and ethical issues over how much is too much. In the quest for knowledge, are we going too far?

Marfan's syndrome is a condition that affects the body. In a child, heart murmurs are an early detection of the condition, although not an absolute one. The skeletal system grows rapidly, causing the vital organs to struggle to keep up. The connective tissue, lacking microfibrils, becomes weak, creating the possibility of a leak or rupture in the aorta over time. Life expectancy varies; some die early, some live seemingly normal lives, even with detection. Without early detection, the only cure is major surgery to repair the aorta, the valve controlling blood flow from the heart.

Often in the news there are reports of a young person actively participating in sports or some other strenuous activity who collapses and dies. It frequently happens and when it does, it saddens the community. This occurs, in part, because schools do not perform thorough physicals for gym or sports participation. It also happens because often the parents are ignorant of these conditions, or if they are aware, they are preoccupied with other matters. As with any ailment, early detection can help increase life expectancy. Without detection, the aorta enlarges, leaks, or ruptures, and heart failure is imminent.

One day before Christmas 1996, DeMal and I were shopping in Livonia, a suburb of Detroit. He was purchasing items for his wife and newborn, while I, having finished most of my shopping, was just browsing. I accompanied him because it was a rare opportunity for us to spend time together. After returning from the Air Force, he took a job with a trucking company, driving as far as California. We spent the whole afternoon together going to three large stores, then he talked me into buying some shoes I was unsure of.

When we got back in the car, DeMal clutched his stomach and chest, grimacing in pain. "What is it? DeMal! Are you all right?!" I wondered if I needed to call an ambulance. *Nothing could be wrong with him*, I thought. *He's the baby. He's young.*

"Hold on. Give me a minute," he said.

I sat there in the passenger seat, questioning what was going on in my baby brother's body, yet I could do nothing. He had complained that he never was the same since the Persian Gulf War. After being vaccinated by the military, he developed rashes on his legs, pains in his joints, dizziness, and skyrocketing blood pressure. I felt the vaccination had done more harm than good.

"DeMal, you okay?" I asked, rubbing his head and shoulder.

"Yeah, I'm all right," he said, regrouping.

I didn't understand how he passed a physical, went through rigorous boot camp training, fought in the Persian Gulf War, and only then was he discharged a year early for health reasons.

"Do you want me to drive?" I asked.

"Nah. I'm straight," he said.

"What is it—gas, indigestion?"

"Seems like indigestion. I'll check with the doctor when I see him next week."

Come to find out he already knew. He was diagnosed when he was discharged from the Air Force. He didn't want me to know that he might die soon; I don't know if it was better or worse for not telling me.

We celebrated Christmas of 1996 with all the family present. DeMal and his wife, Angela, brought their new addition to the family, in addition to the other grandkids, Brit and Corbin. It was baby DeMal's first Christmas and his father's last. Everyone was there. Jim and his three, DeMal and his two, Chyna and me, Mom, even Dad was there. For one who left years ago, he couldn't stay away from his family. He needed us because he was turning into a lonely old man caused by his life choices. He was always welcomed in Mom's house as long as he came in peace.

Linda and her two tall girls were there as well. They weren't taller than DeMal though. They loved DeMal because he kept them and everyone else laughing. He was a big kid with a kid of his own. I could see he was maturing, even though he would always be the baby to me. I never let him forget that I changed his diapers like he was my own kid.

I remember when he was being potty trained. He thought the toilet would flush him away, so he took a poop on the dining room floor instead of using the toilet, then covered it with the vacuum cleaner, thinking we wouldn't find it. What a mess! If he was this clever, it was definitely time for him to use the toilet. Now, it was his turn to experience the joy and frustration of fatherhood. Unlike some, he accepted the challenge and didn't run. He welcomed it, until his very last day.

* * *

Fourteen people gathered around the dining room table. The kids had to eat in the dinette. Mom cooked a feast—turkey and dressing, honey-baked ham, candied yams, turnip greens, macaroni and cheese, giblet gravy, ribs, chicken wings, potato salad, sweet potato pies, and two cakes. This would normally take its toll on an average cook, but Mom started cooking some items weeks before the holiday and froze them.

The large colonial-style house was starting to feel like home again as the stately French Colonial furniture welcomed the guests. The smell of sage permeated the red brick house. A simulated electrical fire burned in the living room's fireplace. The Oriental rugs covered the floors, giving the house a warm and cozy feeling. The artificial green Christmas tree was bursting with color in the corner, while the remnants of opened gifts were scattered about the floor. It looked like Christmas, and Mom wouldn't have had it any other way.

Everyone served themselves liberally in the kitchen and converged on the large, oval dining room table. Dad, eager to eat, loaded his fork with dressing and ate it.

"Hold on. We need to bless the food," Mom said

Everyone bowed their heads.

"Dear Lord. We thank you for the food we are about to receive and ask that You nourish it for human consumption. We thank You for blessing us with the newest addition to our family. Dear Lord, direct our paths so we can be a blessing to him. In Jesus' name we pray. A-men, A-men, and AAAAAA-men," Mom prayed.

"A-men," we said in unison.

After saying grace and blessing the newest addition of the family, we ate heartily, while he drank milk. His little eyes lit up at so much activity. We had a great time. Hours later, everyone left—some with loaded plates. Footsteps in the snow led away from the house in many directions as everyone seemed to go their own way. Christmas hasn't been the same since.

Chapter 21

Late August 1999, I took time out for a day of leisure with two of my closest family, my mother and baby DeMal. We were looking for somewhere near the water to relax because the water had a cooling effect that was so refreshing, making Detroit summers rather pleasant. I was glad my family moved here years ago from the South, but at the same time, I was also glad they had experienced Southern living as well. Few places like Detroit enjoyed the luxury of their own riverfront attached to an international waterway with Canada on the other side. I told anyone who thought they wanted to live here to visit in the winter though. Everybody loved the summer, but the winter can be fierce.

This was a jaunt I often took with Chyna, who became part of my life for the longest time since relocating from Atlanta in 1990. We met at a party on the riverfront when she was home visiting from school. She didn't fit in with the glitz and pretentiousness of the "Wall Street" party, as it was called. That attracted me. In fact, she was wandering around, lost like a child, and looked as if she shouldn't have been there. I grabbed her and asked her to dance. We danced. We talked for a while. I got her number and gave her a hug goodbye because her friends were leaving early. I went somewhere else and met another girl that night because I didn't give Chyna much of a thought at the time. I was on a roll that night. It wasn't until I went to see Chyna a couple of days later that I realized what a treasure I had found. She was pure with no baggage like me and much prettier without her glasses then I had remembered, with her natural "red bone" features.

Chyna's hands were perfectly sculptured and as soft as silk. Her feet, when she let me take her socks off, passed my litmus test with flying colors. They were naturally sculpted with no polish or artificially added nails. Most importantly (although it's all important), she possessed the qualities of women the way they use to make them—with values and a soft-spoken feminine nature. To this day, I have never heard her curse—not once. She was a rare find. It was then that I decided that I wanted to "play in her world" for the longest time.

Chyna and I experienced ten good years together. We both had aging mothers and were the glue that kept everything together. We accepted each other without choosing between our love and family responsibility. I doubt that another woman would have put up with me as long. She was there through some of my struggles. She watched me infiltrate the ranks and move up the corporate ladder in private industry, and she did the same in her field. She went to Hawaii to share the fruits of my labor for seven days and eight tropical nights. She shared my anger when the corporation said they no longer had a place for me. She watched me redeem myself in the court of law. She watched the blueprint of my dreams come to fruition, while some never left the drawing board. She knew my gifts, my strengths, and my weaknesses. Things started changing though.

One day in my new church, Hartford, a lady in red distracted me. As the church sang the benediction hymn, I couldn't wait to ask her name. She had pretty hands and feet too, with red accents. That lady kept my attention for three weeks in restaurants and thirty-five-dollar motels far beyond Detroit's suburbs. If my cell phone could talk (about where I was and what I did when it rang), it would have been ugly. What is said about "a woman's intuition" is real. Without saying a word, Chyna knew something wasn't right. For three weeks, she claimed that I just wasn't all there. She was right. I wasn't there.

Before the year 2000 began, Chyna and I decided to part. Neither of us knew what the millennium had in store, but we chose to meet it independently of each other. She knew I came from a family with a history of divorce, and that in some ways, I was following in my father's footsteps. She knew I had cheated on her at least once.

She wondered if I could ever recoup from my hurt feelings about private industry and work for *them* again, as she wanted me to. She would talk to me, but said I wouldn't listen. I would just stare off into space as if my mind was preoccupied with something else, paying her no mind. It was two years to the day of DeMal's death that I told myself I would never see her again. I was still grieving. In addition to it all, some of her corporate travel was more leisure than I was led to believe. It wasn't like I didn't see it coming.

After years with someone else, I started life on my own and was starting to enjoy it. I came from Atlanta to Detroit, from one relationship to another, with little or no recess, and I was missing something. I needed to fall back in love with myself. I also needed to fall back in love with nature and the spiritual bliss I somehow lost along the way. I was damaged goods now needing repair.

During this outing, I noticed that my mother, the baby, and I were of different generations, but of the same tribe. Mom was about thirty years older than

Kirk Coleman

I was, and I was roughly thirty years older than DeMal at four. Somehow fate brought us together, and we depended on one another, making us a family. We decided to go to Belle Isle, an island that sat in the middle of the Detroit River, connected to the mainland only by a bridge. It was one of Detroit's great treasures that Detroiters often took for granted. However, when visitors come to Detroit, they are amazed by the island and park, surrounded by water, filled with wildlife. We were there because it was quiet in the afternoon, before the teenagers came, and the baby liked to feed the ducks, geese, and deer. We didn't bring the animals food that day.

For some reason, deer were out of their hidden habitat and in full view. There were many groups of deer with different sizes, patterns, color, and gender. People were feeding them; the roadways were blocked with as many as thirty deer in each group. We pulled closer to observe one group of deer, noticing the wide variety of patterns and tried to guess which might be related. Just as we thought we had found a pattern of identification, a "teenage" deer ran across the road. The baby started laughing.

"Look, look!" he laughed excitedly as he stood up in the back, pointing.

"What? What is it?" I asked.

"The deer's got on striped pajamas," he laughed.

I looked at my mother, looked at the deer, and we all got a good laugh from that. The deer had black and white stripes running vertically under his tail all the way to his hind legs that looked like prison stripes. If not for that, he would have fit in with the others.

The deer also came in different sizes. I could see at least three generations of deer. Some were small deer that ran and jumped gleefully. Some were ewe and young bucks with small antlers that grazed and gracefully took handouts from stopping motorists. Some were bucks, the strong, powerful, serious overseers. One stood off in the distance, cautiously watching his herd. When a young deer strayed outside the security of the herd, the buck walked in its direction while lowering his head, revealing the dangerously large antlers. The young deer snapped back into place as if its daddy "pulled off his belt." Unlike some animals, the male deer stayed around after mating to complement the herd. Besides, the only way off the island was crossing a long bridge, so they were stuck there.

"Uncle Kirk, is that the daddy deer?" baby DeMal asked.

"Yeah, man. That's the daddy deer. He's doing just what a daddy deer is supposed to do."

I drove off to find what else we could see. As we cruised around the island finishing off our lunches, the breeze came off Lake St. Clair, clearing my lungs, cooling us off, and literally separated my loose-fitting clothes from my body. The crisp September sun radiated off the water in blinding proportions, indicating the possibility of an Indian summer. The trees crackled with movement while the leaves held on tightly, knowing it was yet too soon to let go. *This could have been any day in May, June, or July*, I thought. It was a pleasant, perfect day that all of my senses welcomed acutely. I was cautious, however, because I learned that a good day couldn't be determined until the day's end.

We had almost circled the five-mile island completely and were nearing the golf course that marked the last mile. Off to my left, I came upon one of the biggest bucks I have ever seen and stopped in the road so we could watch. He was a hunter's prize, although, not being a hunter, I didn't consider him as such. I looked at the animal in amazement as he looked over curiously at me—eye to eye. As baby DeMal was moving some bags around in the back, the deer, with his keen hearing, approached slowly until he stuck his head in the window, looking for food just inches from my face. Somehow the animal knew we would do him no harm. We had nothing to give him though, but I patted him on his head.

"Hold on, deer. I'll be back," I said.

I sped off, crossed the bridge, found a store, and returned with three loaves of wheat bread. I went back to the same place looking for the deer, but he was not there.

Approximately two city blocks up the road, I saw the deer and many, many others like him. There must have been fifty deer in this group walking slowly. They were of different gender, colors, and sizes, but they were deer just the same. At the time they all appeared to be dark cocoa brown or tawny colored, with an array of patterns, too many to follow. I stopped in the middle of the road, and the deer converged on my car, coming from all directions. I cracked the windows so we could feed them the wheat bread. After feeding the hungry bucks for a while, I thought it was time to spread the wealth. I tossed the bread out further so the other deer in the hierarchy could eat as well.

Over to the side, I saw a white deer that stood out from the rest. Using a piece of wheat bread, I beckoned it closer and threw it in its direction. The deer approached the bread, but it turned away as though ashamed as another deer came and scooped it up. I shooed away a big buck at the window while repeating the same process. The white deer seemed afraid to eat, although it appeared it wanted to. Why was the deer programmed to think that it couldn't eat? Did it think that because it was white, it was inferior to the others?

My curiosity turned to irritation as I opened the door, got out the car, and tried to feed the white deer the wheat bread. It turned away. Another deer ate it every time. Could it be the wheat bread? Did the white deer prefer white bread?

Closely examining the deer, I could see it was the runt of the herd. Looking at its rear end, I could see it was pinkish and worn from other deer ramming it with their antlers or biting on it. It obviously was the kicking board of the herd because it was different from the others. It was white. Why didn't it move on to another herd? There were other deer on the island. In this case, being alone was not so bad.

I passed out the remainder of the second loaf of bread and left all the deer standing in the road. I challenged nature. Nature won. I felt sorry for the white deer, fearing it may starve, but I had tried to feed it. I had another loaf of wheat bread that we decided was needed at home for human consumption. I had planned to feed all three loaves to the animals until the deer spoiled it for themselves. I would have given them all the bread I had, but I was distracted by their actions. I often wondered if God reacts to me the same way.

Epilogue

A year later, the fall of 2000, and civilized life, as we know it, still existed—for now. The year came and was almost gone without the much expected doom and gloom of Y2K prophets, although my third eye did detect cracks in the foundation. Leaving all trivialities aside, I was determined to live and enjoy life and not be troubled with microscopic details. I would focus on what I could see with my very own eyes.

I already had worked about a year in my new job in the public sector, solving my dilemma with employment in the private industry for now. I was learning to use my gifts selectively. I had a new car that I drove to the family reunion in Atlanta after I dropped Mom and the baby off in Birmingham, Alabama. After three days of enjoyment in Atlanta, I picked them up in Birmingham and took them back to Atlanta, where we spent the night in a fancy hotel and toured the area the next morning. When I got back to Detroit, I would see Chyna because we were still talking and agreed to see each other once again.

I had more responsibility than ever with baby DeMal and was memorizing the price of a Happy Meal, plus tax. I found myself watching cartoons instead of the Food Network and playing video games even when DeMal wasn't around. I was the closest he had to a father, and he was like a son to me. I am his father's blood. Although I will never let him forget who his real Dad was, I wanted him to have every opportunity to grow, knowing the world was his apple, regardless of what he lacked.

That Sunday evening when we arrived in Atlanta, I drove up to the Martin Luther King Memorial site which I remembered being in one of the toughest parts of the city, Auburn Avenue, now under major renovation. I drove up, parked alongside it, and saw the eternal flame from the street. I got out of the car and took the baby with me, while Mom stayed there and caught the view from the car. We walked up the steps and viewed the memorial site as I prepared myself for the barrage of questions that I knew would follow.

"Uncle Kirk, what's that?" he asked.

"That's the burial place of Martin Luther King Jr."

"Did he die?"

"Yes, he died years ago."

"Is he in there now?"

"Well, his remains are ... his body is there, but his spirit is gone."

"Uncle Kirk, where did his spirit go?"

"His spirit went to heaven where God lives, and his spirit is with you and me—just like your dad."

"Listen," I added, trying not to make this any more complex than it must have been for a four-year-old child. "If anyone asks you about Martin Luther King Jr., just remember that he changed the world. So what did Martin Luther King Jr. do?" I asked.

"He changed the world," the baby said.

"Good. Let's go."

I delicately cupped his small head with my large hands and steered him away towards the car. He hopped and skipped away. I know he'll never forget what I told him that day. As he grows, he will experience for himself what he previewed that day in Atlanta along with many, many other experiences. Each experience will bring questions. One day, I hope to be the "wise old man" to help steer him along the way.

BOOK AVAILABLE THROUGH
Milligan Books, Inc.

Sinz of The Fatha $14.95

Order Form

Milligan Books, Inc.
1425 W. Manchester Ave., Suite C
Los Angeles, CA 90047
(323) 750-3592

Name_____ Date _____
Address_____
City_____ State____ Zip Code ____
Day Telephone _____
Evening Telephone _____
Book Title _____
Number of books ordered___ Total ....$ _____
Sales Taxes (CA Add 8.25%).....................$ _____
Shipping & Handling $4.90 for one book ..$ _____
Add $1.00 for each additional book ....$ _____
Total Amount Due.....................................$ _____
☐ Check ☐ Money Order ☐ Other Cards _____
☐ Visa   ☐ MasterCard Expiration Date _____
Credit Card No. _____
Driver License No. _____

Make check payable to Milligan Books, Inc.

_____   _____
Signature   Date